MACMILLAN MASTER GUIDES

KIM

BY RUDYARD KIPLING

LEONÉE ORMOND

© Leonée Ormond 1988

All rights reserved. No reproduction, copy or transmission of this publication may be made without written permission.

No paragraph of this publication may be reproduced, copied or transmitted save with written permission or in accordance with the provisions of the Copyright Act 1956 (as amended), or under the terms of any licence permitting limited copying issued by the Copyright Licensing Agency, 33-4 Alfred Place, London WC1E 7DP.

Any person who does any unauthorised act in relation to this publication may be liable to criminal prosecution and civil claims for damages.

First edition 1988

Published by
MACMILLAN EDUCATION LTD
Houndmills, Basingstoke, Hampshire RG2 2XS
and London
Companies and representatives
throughout the world

Printed in Hong Kong

British Library Cataloguing in Publication Data
Ormond, Leonée
Kim, by Rudyard Kipling.—(Macmillan
master guides).
1. Kipling, Rudyard. Kim
I. Title II. Kipling, Rudyard
823'.8   PR4854.K4
ISBN 0-333-43849-3 Pbk
ISBN 0-333-43802-7 Pbk export

MACMILLAN MASTER GUIDES

GENERAL EDITOR: JAMES GIBSON

JANE AUSTEN	*Emma* Norman Page
	Sense and Sensibility Judy Simons
	Persuasion Judy Simons
	Pride and Prejudice Raymond Wilson
	Mansfield Park Richard Wirdnam
SAMUEL BECKETT	*Waiting for Godot* Jennifer Birkett
WILLIAM BLAKE	*Songs of Innocence* and *Songs of Experience* Alan Tomlinson
ROBERT BOLT	*A Man for All Seasons* Leonard Smith
CHARLOTTE BRONTË	*Jane Eyre* Robert Miles
EMILY BRONTË	*Wuthering Heights* Hilda D. Spear
JOHN BUNYAN	*The Pilgrim's Progress* Beatrice Batson
GEOFFREY CHAUCER	*The Miller's Tale* Michael Alexander
	The Pardoner's Tale Geoffrey Lester
	The Wife of Bath's Tale Nicholas Marsh
	The Knight's Tale Anne Samson
	The Prologue to the Canterbury Tales Nigel Thomas and Richard Swan
JOSEPH CONRAD	*The Secret Agent* Andrew Mayne
CHARLES DICKENS	*Bleak House* Dennis Butts
	Great Expectations Dennis Butts
	Hard Times Norman Page
GEORGE ELIOT	*Middlemarch* Graham Handley
	Silas Marner Graham Handley
	The Mill on the Floss Helen Wheeler
T. S. ELIOT	*Murder in the Cathedral* Paul Lapworth
	Selected Poems Andrew Swarbrick
HENRY FIELDING	*Joseph Andrews* Trevor Johnson
E. M. FORSTER	*Howards End* Ian Milligan
	A Passage to India Hilda D. Spear
WILLIAM GOLDING	*The Spire* Rosemary Sumner
	Lord of the Flies Raymond Wilson
OLIVER GOLDSMITH	*She Stoops to Conquer* Paul Ranger
THOMAS HARDY	*The Mayor of Casterbridge* Ray Evans
	Tess of the d'Urbervilles James Gibson
	Far from the Madding Crowd Colin Temblett-Wood
BEN JONSON	*Volpone* Michael Stout
JOHN KEATS	*Selected Poems* John Garrett
RUDYARD KIPLING	*Kim* Leonée Ormond

MACMILLAN MASTER GUIDES

PHILIP LARKIN	*The Whitsun Weddings* and *The Less Deceived* Andrew Swarbrick
D. H. LAWRENCE	*Sons and Lovers* R. P. Draper
HARPER LEE	*To Kill a Mockingbird* Jean Armstrong
LAURIE LEE	*Cider with Rosie* Brian Tarbitt
GERARD MANLEY HOPKINS	*Selected Poems* R. J. C. Watt
CHRISTOPHER MARLOWE	*Doctor Faustus* David A. Male
THE METAPHYSICAL POETS	Joan van Emden
THOMAS MIDDLETON and WILLIAM ROWLEY	*The Changeling* Tony Bromham
ARTHUR MILLER	*The Crucible* Leonard Smith *Death of a Salesman* Peter Spalding
GEORGE ORWELL	*Animal Farm* Jean Armstrong
WILLIAM SHAKESPEARE	*Richard II* Charles Barber *Othello* Tony Bromham *Hamlet* Jean Brooks *King Lear* Francis Casey *Henry V* Peter Davison *The Winter's Tale* Diana Devlin *Julius Caesar* David Elloway *Macbeth* David Elloway *The Merchant of Venice* A. M. Kinghorn *Measure for Measure* Mark Lilly *Henry IV Part I* Helen Morris *Romeo and Juliet* Helen Morris *A Midsummer Night's Dream* Kenneth Pickering *The Tempest* Kenneth Pickering *Coriolanus* Gordon Williams *Antony and Cleopatra* Martin Wine
GEORGE BERNARD SHAW	*St Joan* Leonée Ormond
RICHARD SHERIDAN	*The School for Scandal* Paul Ranger *The Rivals* Jeremy Rowe
ALFRED TENNYSON	*In Memoriam* Richard Gill
EDWARD THOMAS	*Selected Poems* Gerald Roberts
ANTHONY TROLLOPE	*Barchester Towers* K. M. Newton
JOHN WEBSTER	*The White Devil* and *The Duchess of Malfi* David A. Male
VIRGINIA WOOLF	*To the Lighthouse* John Mepham *Mrs Dalloway* Julian Pattison
WILLIAM WORDSWORTH	*The Prelude Books I and II* Helen Wheeler

CONTENTS

General editor's preface   *vii*

Acknowledgements   *viii*

1 Life
- 1.1 Early years — 1
- 1.2 The genesis of *Kim* — 4
- 1.3 Later years — 4

2 Plot synopsis and critical commentary — 6

3 Themes, issues and background
- 3.1 India in the later nineteenth century — 27
- 3.2 The geography of *Kim* — 29
- 3.3 Racial division — 29
- 3.4 Religious division — 32
- 3.5 Dress — 37
- 3.6 Spoken language — 38
- 3.7 Written language — 41
- 3.8 Learning and knowing — 42
- 3.9 Parent and child — 43
- 3.10 Identity — 45
- 3.11 The secret group — 47
- 3.12 The Great Game — 49

4 Technical features
- 4.1 Picaresque — 51
- 4.2 *Bildungsroman* — 52
- 4.3 The adventure story — 53
- 4.4 Realism — 55
- 4.5 Characterisation — 56
- 4.6 Narration — 62
- 4.7 Kipling's prose — 62
- 4.8 Audience — 66

5	**Specimen passage and commentary**	5.1	Specimen passage	68
		5.2	Commentary	70
6	**Critical reception**	6.1	Contemporary reviews	73
		6.2	Later criticisms	75

Revision questions 80

Further reading 82

GENERAL EDITOR'S PREFACE

The aim of the Macmillan Master Guides is to help you to appreciate the book you are studying by providing information about it and by suggesting ways of reading and thinking about it which will lead to a fuller understanding. The section on the writer's life and background has been designed to illustrate those aspects of the writer's life which have influenced the work, and to place it in its personal and literary context. The summaries and critical commentary are of special importance in that each brief summary of the action is followed by an examination of the significant critical points. The space which might have been given to repetitive explanatory notes has been devoted to a detailed analysis of the kind of passage which might confront you in an examination. Literary criticism is concerned with both the broader aspects of the work being studied and with its detail. The ideas which meet us in reading a great work of literature, and their relevance to us today, are an essential part of our study, and our Guides look at the thought of their subject in some detail. But just as essential is the craft with which the writer has constructed his work of art, and this may be considered under several technical headings – characterisation, language, style and stagecraft, for example.

The authors of these Guides are all teachers and writers of wide experience, and they have chosen to write about books they admire and know well in the belief that they can communicate their admiration to you. But you yourself must read and know intimately the book you are studying. No one can do that for you. You should see this book as a lamp-post. Use it to shed light, not to lean against. If you know your text and know what it is saying about life, and how it says it, then you will enjoy it, and there is no better way of passing an examination in literature.

JAMES GIBSON

ACKNOWLEDGEMENTS

The edition of *Kim* to which reference is made throughout this guide is that first published by St Martin's Library in 1961, and republished by Pan Books, in association with Macmillan London Ltd in 1976. It is widely available in paperback. The bracketed numbers throughout the text refer to page numbers of the Pan edition, 1976.

I am grateful to Mr B. M. Chaudhuri for help in disentangling the languages of Northern India.

My thanks go to my husband, Richard, for discussing my text with me, and to my elder son, Augustus, for sharing his thoughts on *Kim*. I recall with pleasure a conversation with my brother-in-law, David Housego, at a very early stage in my work, when his great enthusiasm for *Kim* was an immense encouragement. At a later stage, I consulted Jenny Housego, Jemima Pitman and Michael Archer, all of whom were prepared to share their considerable knowledge of India. Dr. Mildred Archer and Miss Betty Tyers gave valuable help with picture research.

I end with an affectionate acknowledgement of my nephew, Kim Housego, whose name certainly entitles him to a special mention here.

Leonée Ormond

Cover illustration: *A Street in Lahore – Punjab* by William Carpenter, by courtesy of the Victoria and Albert Museum.

1 LIFE

1.1. EARLY YEARS

Rudyard Kipling was born in Bombay on 30 December 1865, son of John Lockwood Kipling and of his wife, Alice, née Macdonald. Both the boy's grandfathers were Methodist ministers, which may help to account for the Biblical flavour of his prose. Of his mother's sisters, two married distinguished artists, Edward Burne Jones (1833–98) and Edward Poynter (1836–1919), and another became the mother of a Conservative prime minister, Stanley Baldwin (1867–1947). At the time of Kipling's birth, his father, a designer and craftsman, had recently been appointed to a teaching post at the Bombay School of Art. A second child, 'Trix', was born in 1868.

The Kiplings were in England in 1868, and again in 1871. On this second visit, they abruptly left the children, Rudyard being nearly 6, as paying guests with a retired captain and his wife, the Holloways. Brother and sister remained in Southsea, without seeing their parents, until 1877. After a happy and indulged boyhood in India, the change to English lower-middle-class life was traumatic. As long as Captain Holloway lived, Rudyard enjoyed some protection from the severe and puritanical 'Aunty Rosa' and her son, Harry, but after the Captain's death in 1874, he was entirely at their mercy. Mrs Holloway was fond of Trix, but formed an intense dislike for Rudyard. The only relief from his misery came on the annual holidays he spent with the Burne Jones family in Fulham.

Kipling told the story of his ill-treatment by Mrs Holloway in a short story, 'Baa, Baa, Black Sheep' (1888) and in his first novel, *The Light that Failed* (1890). In his posthumously published autobiography, *Something of Myself* (1937), he made it clear that these were his own experiences. The Southsea episode had a profound psychological effect upon the boy, not least because of the hell-fire and damnation with which his tormentor threatened him. The memory of this sudden change from an atmosphere of love to one of hostility must lie behind Kipling's account of Kim's desolation, when, deprived of the lama, he is subjected to the chill loneliness of the empty British barracks at Umballa.

It was accepted practice for parents in India to send their children home, but not usually to strangers, nor for so long without visiting them. In *The Strange Ride of Rudyard Kipling*, Angus Wilson convincingly analyses the professional pressures which led the Kiplings to remain in India. Kipling himself seems never to have blamed his parents, and his close relationship with his sister did something to ameliorate his despair. In his autobiography he writes of the positive results of the experience: 'In the long run these things, and many more of the like, drained me of any capacity for real, personal hate for the rest of my days.' How true this is has been disputed, for hatred and a desire for revenge are intermittent features of Kipling's writing.

Kipling's mother returned to England in 1877. There is a vivid account of their first meeting. Seeing her approach, her son put up his arm to ward off the anticipated blow. In the following year he became a pupil at United Services College, Westward Ho!, Devon. Kipling deeply admired the headmaster, Cormell Price, an old friend of Burne Jones, and a liberal. Kipling's schoolboy friendships with L. C. Dunsterville (Stalky) and George Beresford (M'Turk) later inspired *Stalky and Co.* (1899).

Most boys from the school went into the army, or on to university. The Kiplings could not afford higher education, and Rudyard left school in 1882, at the age of 16. In the autumn of that year, he returned to India, where his father was now Principal of the School of Art and Curator of the Central Museum in Lahore. Kipling lived at home and worked as a journalist on the *Lahore Civil and Military Gazette*. In 1887 he joined another paper, *The Pioneer*, in Allahabad. Kipling's work as a journalist gave him the detailed knowledge of Indian life which is so abundantly displayed in *Kim*. Rumours of Russian infiltration were a frequent subject of discussion, and family holidays in the hill resort of Simla, travels in the north and along the Grand Trunk Road, all provided background material for the novel.

Kipling published a volume of poems, *Departmental Ditties*, in 1886, and a collection of stories, *Plain Tales from the Hills*, in 1888. By the time he returned to England in 1889, he was already on his way to becoming a literary celebrity. His first novel, *The Light that Failed*, reflects the strains of London life. In the year of its publication, 1890, Kipling, suffering from overwork, set out on a round-the-world voyage, which took him to India for the last time.

It was while he was there that he heard the tragic news of the death of the young American writer, Wolcott Balestier, with whom he had collaborated in the writing of a joint novel, *The Naulahka* (1892). He hastily returned to London, and, in 1892, married his friend's sister, Caroline. The reasons for the marriage are not entirely clear, but in the view of one of Kipling's biographers, Charles Carrington, it was 'bound up with his devotion to Wolcott'.

Kipling and his wife settled down near her family home at Brattleboro in Vermont, and their daughters, Josephine and Elsie, were born there. Many of Kipling's finest stories date from his American years, among them two volumes of *The Jungle Book* (1894-5). There are clear parallels between the story of Kim, the British boy who lives as an Indian, and that of Mowgli, the man-cub who lives in the animal world.

The Kiplings left Vermont in 1896 after a disastrous quarrel with Caroline's brother, Beatty, culminating in a lawsuit when Kipling accused his brother-in-law of trying to kill him. The Kiplings went first to Torquay, and then to Rottingdean in Sussex, close to Edward Burne Jones. John Kipling was born there in 1897. In the same year, *Captains Courageous*, another novel about a boy finding himself, was published.

In 1899, the Kiplings crossed the Atlantic once more. On their arrival in New York, Kipling became seriously ill and, before he was out of danger, his daughter, Josephine, died from pneumonia. This, probably the most traumatic event of Kipling's adult life, was a blow from which he never recovered.

1.2 THE GENESIS OF *KIM*

In July 1885, Kipling wrote to his aunt, Edith Macdonald, from Simla, telling her that he had written 237 pages of an Indian novel, 'Mother Maturin': 'It's not one bit nice or proper but carries a grim sort of moral with it and tries to deal with the unutterable horrors of lower-class Eurasian and native life as they exist outside reports and reports and reports.' A friend later described the plot: 'It is the story of an old Irishwoman who kept an opium den in Lahore but sent her daughter to be educated in England. She married a Civilian and came to live in Lahore – hence a story how Government secrets came to be known in the Bazaar and *vice versa*.' The theme of 'Mother Maturin' continued to grow, but when Kipling left India for London in 1889, it was still incomplete.

While living in Vermont, Kipling began to consider the idea of turning 'Mother Maturin' into something else. As the manuscript of the early novel no longer exists, it is impossible to be sure how much was carried over, but *Kim* is evidently cast in a more cheerful vein than its predecessor. The character of Kim first came to him in Vermont: 'I had a vague notion of an Irish boy, born in India and mixed up with native life. I went as far as to make him the son of a private in an Irish Battalion, and christened him "Kim of the 'Rishti" – short, that is, for Irish.' It was to be eight years before the novel was finished.

In his autobiography, Kipling tells of many conversations he held with his father on the subject of Indian life, required as background for *Kim*, his last treatment of an Indian subject. Lockwood Kipling appears as a character in the novel, and, appropriately, he illustrated the first book edition of 1901.

The novel was published in America in *McClure's Magazine* from December 1900 to October 1901, and in England in *Cassell's Magazine* from January to November 1901.

1.3 LATER YEARS

In 1902, Kipling moved to his final home, Batemans, Burwash, Sussex. Some of his most profound and most moving stories date from the Sussex period. *Puck of Pook's Hill* (1906), *Rewards and*

Fairies (1910), 'They' (1904) and 'The Wish House' (1926) all draw directly upon the landscape and people of Sussex.

Kipling's son, John, died in the First World War, and after the war his father devoted a great deal of time to the Imperial War Graves Commission. Kipling became known as a conservative, and as an upholder of ideas of empire. Towards the end of his life, his attitudes became anathema to liberals and literary critics alike. His public popularity, however, never waned. As his writing abundantly demonstrates, Kipling was a far more divided and thoughtful man than he seemed. He was awarded the Nobel Prize for Literature in 1907, but refused all other honours. He died in 1936.

2 PLOT SYNOPSIS AND CRITICAL COMMENTARY

CHAPTER 1

Synopsis

Kim opens in Lahore, the capital city of the Punjab, then a province in Northern India and now in Pakistan. Kimball O'Hara, a boy of 13, sits outside the Lahore Museum, astride a Mohammedan gun, Zam-Zammah. The boy's parents are dead: his mother, a former nursemaid, died when he was 3, his Irish father, a soldier turned railway-worker, seven years later. His father's only legacy to Kim is the amulet with Masonic papers which hangs round the boy's neck. Kim lives with an Indian woman, and passes his time in the streets of Lahore. Dressed sometimes in European, sometimes in Hindu or Mohammedan clothes, the boy, known as 'Little Friend of all the World', mixes freely with all castes and races.

An old Tibetan lama approaches and asks whether he can enter the museum. Kim, fascinated by the stranger, follows him inside and watches the lama's meeting with the curator. The lama explains that he has come to India to see the holy places of the Buddhist faith. More important, he is searching for an unknown sacred river. When he entered an archery contest to win a bride, the Buddha's falling arrow became the source of a river. By entering it, a man can escape from the turning wheel of reincarnation and achieve nirvana. The curator shows the lama photographs and maps of the sacred places, but cannot tell him where the river is.

Kim decides to accompany the lama to the holy city of Benares. While the lama sleeps, Kim changes into Hindu clothes. Assuming the role of the holy man's chela, or disciple, he takes the lama to the Kashmir Serai, a resting-place for travellers. At the Serai, Kim meets Mahbub Ali, a Pathan, or Afghan, horse-dealer, for whom he has acted as a spy. Hearing of Kim's journey to Benares, Mahbub pays him to deliver a secret message to Umballa, ostensibly about the pedigree of a horse. The narrator tells the reader that Mahbub is a British agent and that the secret service are anxious to learn more about Russian incursions into the northern border area. Having given Kim the vital document, Mahbub goes to a brothel, where he drinks heavily and is searched. Kim, meanwhile, sees a man turning out Mahbub's belongings in the Serai. Sensing danger, Kim leaves with the lama.

Commentary

Most of the chapters of *Kim* are prefaced with a quotation from Kipling's own poems. At the head of the first three chapters stand verses from 'Buddha at Kamakura'. The verse here contrasts the 'narrow way' of Christianity, with the 'heathen' Buddhism of the shrine of Kamakura in Japan. The poet tells the reader to exercise tolerance:

> Be gentle when 'the heathen' pray
> To Buddha at Kamakura (7).

The lama and his 'alien' faith are a positive spiritual force in the novel, and the stress on the Buddha's progress towards enlightenment is a structural corollary for Kim's very different progress towards understanding himself.

The opening chapter of *Kim* introduces both main elements of the plot: the lama's quest and the 'Great Game' of the British secret service. Both involve travel out of Lahore, but Kim's decision to leave with the lama has been taken before he agrees to deliver Mahbub Ali's message.

The chapter opens with the humorous treatment of deep religious and racial divisions in India. The gun, Zam-Zammah, is a symbol of conquest: 'for the great green-bronze piece is always first of the conqueror's loot' (7). Kim, as the representative of the most recent conquerors, the British, prevents both the Moslem and the Hindu boy from climbing onto the gun. Only when the lama appears does he climb down. Where the other boys reject the lama as alien, Kim, who is free of religious intolerance, is curious and well-intentioned towards the old man.

The meeting between the lama and the curator introduces ideas of harmony. Through a common appreciation of Buddhist sculpture, the two men are able to cross the barriers of race and religion, and to communicate. An exchange of gifts symbolises their relationship. The curator gives the lama his spectacles, together with a notebook and pencils, with which the old man can draw the wheel of existence. The lama responds by giving the curator his ancient Chinese pen-case: 'We be craftsmen together, thou and I.' (18). The limits of such a relationship, dependent upon art and learning, are established by the curator's apologetic admission that he does not know the whereabouts of the lama's holy river.

This first chapter also states the theme of fatherhood, with the introduction of Kipling's own father, in the guise of the curator, and of the lama and Mahbub Ali, both father-figures to the boy. Like the lama, Mahbub believes that Kim has been sent by providence, so that, on this occasion at least, both fathers send the boy in the same direction.

Kim's mastery of his environment is established from the first sentence. He is able to go into all parts of the city, is skilled in 'intrigue', and is clever in finding food and shelter for the lama. His response to the threatening scene with which the chapter ends reveals courage and intelligence as well as experience: 'he had known all evil since he could speak' (9).

CHAPTER 2

Synopsis

Kim and the lama arrive at the crowded Lahore railway station. Kim buys the lama a ticket to Umballa, but only pays his own fare to Amritzar. The compartment is crowded with people, representing many of the religious groups of Northern India. They discuss differences in social and religious practices. At Amritzar, Kim persuades a prostitute to pay his fare to Umballa. The passengers, relaxing, talk of the lama's quest and of the red bull on a green field, a cryptic description passed on to Kim by his father which he believes to be his own inheritance.

At Umballa, a passenger, the cultivator's wife, invites Kim and the lama to the house of her husband's cousin. Having established the lama there, Kim delivers his message at Colonel Creighton's bungalow. He hides in order to observe the repercussions. He sees the Commander-in-Chief arrive and hears him issue orders to mobilise forces for a punitive raid on the disloyal rulers of the north.

On his return, Kim finds the lama discussing horoscopes with their hosts' family priest. The priest tells Kim that he will find his bull within three days. In the morning, the lama and Kim leave, intending to walk to Benares,

Commentary

Chapter 2 is headed with another verse from 'Buddha at Kamakura', again commending the virtue of religious tolerance. Those who abandon pride 'May feel the Soul of all the East . . . at Kamakura' (34).

Although the poem is directed at a British reader, the chapter itself explores religious and caste differences among the peoples of India. The train passengers and the family party in the house of the cultivator's cousin are preoccupied with the pros and cons of various religions. They observe that British rule has broken down barriers. Regiments and railway trains have both thrown castes, races and sexes together in an unprecedented manner.

The chapter further demonstrates Kim's knowingness, and his care for the unworldly lama as they pursue what are already presented as related personal quests, one for peace, the other for war:

'Tck! Armed men – many hundreds. What concern hast thou with war?' said the priest to Kim. 'Thine is a red and angry sign of War to be loosed very soon.'
'None – none,' said the lama earnestly. 'We seek only peace and our River' (49).

Knowledge and innocence are wittily contrasted in the scene when Kim chooses to beg from a prostitute. When his intuition that she will give proves correct, the lama supposes her to be a nun. The prostitute is no Mary Magdalen, but the lama's response to her generosity is the right one. His human warmth again undermines his 'rule' when, in his pleasure at telling travellers' tales of Tibet, the lama forgets the forbidden presence of a woman in his audience.

In the scene when Kim delivers the message to Colonel Creighton, Kipling makes him the observer of events he does not wholly understand. British reactions to Mahbub Ali's note involve the reader in a spate of unknown names and of unfamiliar concepts. Like Kim, we cannot expect to have more than a general conception of the strategy: 'they will loose a great army to punish some one – somewhere – the news goes to Pindi and Peshawur. There are also guns. Would I had crept nearer' (47).

CHAPTER 3

Synopsis

Kim and the lama walk through the outskirts of Umballa. A market gardener reviles them as beggars, then changes his tune because he fears that the lama will put a curse on his crops. Kim is frightened by a cobra, but the lama persuades him to go past it, insisting that it is a part of creation.

At evening, Kim and the lama come to a village where they describe their quest to a group of headmen. Kim confidently predicts that a war is coming, and a retired native captain, a Rissaldar, invites him to stay for the night. The Hindu priest entertains the lama. Kim first borrows the lama's money, rightly suspecting that the priest plans to drug and rob the old man. In the morning, the old soldier accompanies Kim and the lama to the Grand Trunk Road, talking of his loyal service in the Indian mutiny of 1857. On the road one of his three sons is seen haranguing the driver of a broken-down cart. The chapter ends with the embrace of a father and son.

Commentary

Chapter 3 gives an account of the journey of the lama and Kim. As in the picaresque (journey) fiction of Henry Fielding (1701–54), the pair have humorous and dangerous experiences. The market gardener first displays anger, and then, nervous about the threat to his livelihood, offers water and milk. He is contrasted with the cobra, which, although truly dangerous, is content to drink from the river and rest on the bank, ignoring the travellers as they go past him. The lama takes a generous view of both. The worldly Kim has to protect the innocent lama against the wiles of the priest, an Indian equivalent of the rascally innkeeper of picaresque fiction. It is in any case appropriate to the war/peace dichotomy that Kim should lodge with a soldier and the lama with a priest.

The simplicity of the lama is the source for much irony throughout the book. He is described, even by Kim, as 'mad', but the lama can see more clearly than the 'sane' characters. The opening verse, an early version of 'Buddha at Kamakura', tells of those souls who cling to the rungs of life, and so cannot escape from the cycle of rebirth. The Hindu priest, planning a robbery; the old soldier whose only regret is his failing strength, and whose mind still runs on the loyalties and betrayals of the mutiny; Kim, with his conceited delight at his knowledge of the coming war; all three are still 'bound to the wheel'.

Within the chapter are a series of counter arguments, suggesting the virtues of the world of action. The old soldier's memories of the mutiny take on the quality of myth. When he sings of John Nicholson, Nikal Seyn, a figure of heroic stature, the lama and Kim are enthralled, although the lama tries to conceal it. Most revealing of the divisions within the lama is the passage where he and the soldier fall asleep under a tree. A small boy disturbs them, and is frightened. The lama comforts the child by singing to it, a 'natural' and kindly action of which the lama, bent on renouncing human feeling, is ashamed, but which commends him to the old soldier and to the reader.

CHAPTER 4

Synopsis

The old soldier's son gives Kim money, and a policeman tries unsuccessfully to extract a road tax from him. The narrator describes Kim's delight in watching the travellers along the Grand Trunk Road, while the lama, lost in thought, ignores his surroundings. At evening, the travellers arrive at a camping ground, where Kim notices the bullock-cart of a rich widow from the north. He manages to attract her attention, and, deeply respecting the lama, she provides food and bedding, and then suggests that he join her party. She requests a charm to ensure a second son for her daughter. In the morning, Kim and the lama leave with her.

Commentary

In one of his finest pieces of prose, Kipling evokes the colours, sounds and smells of India. The account of different castes and groups upon the Grand Trunk Road further develops his presentation of a deeply divided land, its discordant elements drawn together through the observing and unprejudiced eye of the observer, Kim.

The plot progresses only through the meeting with the Ranee, the lucky chance referred to in the introductory poem. Even the conflicts of world and spirit, war and religion, are less prominent here than in the earlier chapters. Humour is dominant. The Ranee, who should be in purdah (secluded), is on pilgrimage. Like the Prioress in Chaucer's *Canterbury Tales*, she is really enjoying a holiday. The narrator wryly comments that families often found it restful to send such powerful old women away for a time. At her age, she no longer needs to hide her face from men, and even engages in a lively dialogue with an English superintendent of police. (This figure is later revealed to be Strickland, a leading member of the secret service, and a character in other stories by Kipling.) The Ranee's pilgrimage contrasts directly with the lama's, but, for a time, their journeys are combined, like the two 'quests' of Kim and the lama. The lama asks Kim: 'Is there any reason against? I can still step aside and try all the rivers that the road over-passes. She desires that I should come. She very greatly desires it' (84).

CHAPTER 5

Synopsis

Kim and the lama, in the train of the Ranee, set up camp for the night. Kim, curious as ever, walks off to explore the surrounding country, and the lama follows him. They watch as two men run up a flag showing a red bull on a green ground. A British regiment, the Mavericks, is about to make camp. Kim believes this to be the fulfilment of the Umballa priest's prophecy, and decides to come back after dinner.

On his return, Kim leaves the lama at a distance, and watches the regimental dinner through the tent door. The Church of England clergyman, Arthur Bennett, leaving the tent after the loyal toast, trips over the boy. Trying to capture Kim, Bennett breaks the chain round his neck, and discovers the papers in the amulet. From these, Bennett and the Roman Catholic chaplain, Father Victor, establish Kim's parentage. They decide that he is a regimental orphan and that the regiment must educate him. Kim intends to escape at once, but the lama says that he will pay for the boy's education at St Xavier's in Lucknow. The lama blames himself for feeling worldly affection. After the departure of the lama, Kim declares that the regiment is about to go to war. He is not believed.

Commentary

Chapter 5 is one of the most dramatic episodes in *Kim*. Up to this point the plot has been largely concerned with the relationship of Kim and the lama, and with their quest for the river of enlightenment. Until now, connections with the British have seemed tangential rather than central, and the delivery of the message a separate incident.

But now, almost as soon as the travellers have settled into a comfortable haven provided by the Ranee, Kim's meeting with his father's regiment draws him abruptly away from the lama. He does not rejoin him until Chapter 11, three years later. If the opening chapters are largely concerned with native India, those in the middle deal with British India. Chapter 5 is the pivot which shifts us from one world to the other.

By the end of the chapter, Kim has been translated to an entirely new environment, his third in as many days. The run of events which precipitates him into the embrace of the Mavericks is even more startling than that which takes him away from Lahore with the lama in Chapter 1. In what Father Victor sees as a 'miracle', the boy is recognised as white, and thus becomes subject to a different code of behaviour. Bennett's change of attitude when he realises Kim's parentage lies at the heart of the book's discussion of race: 'It is possible I have done the boy an injustice. He is certainly white' (97–8).

The chapter, particularly in its later stages, is characterised by lack of understanding and communication. The dialogue between Bennett, Father Victor, the lama and Kim is a closely worked exposition of four different voices, differentiated by timbre and intonation as well as by philosophy. Kim, by far the youngest, and the only non-churchman, acts as interpreter for the others, and, through the power of tongues, assumes the power of manipulation. Kim's one aim is to run away quickly, and to rejoin his master. Like the prodigal son in the wry poem which heads the chapter, he would rather return to what, by British standards, are the 'pigs' and the 'styes' (89). He reckons, however, without the force of the lama's love for him. The lama, seeing further than he, understands the implications of what he hears: 'A Sahib and the son of a Sahib' (103). He decides to pay for Kim's education, to rescue the boy from the racial limbo into which he has fallen, and to establish him with the identity appropriate to his station. Sonship is again important here. Kim is returned to the regiment through his natural father's agency, and he is temporarily 'abandoned' by his surrogate father, the lama.

CHAPTER 6

Synopsis

The Mavericks are called away north to the war. Kim is left behind in the barracks at Umballa, guarded by a drummer-boy. He sends a letter to Mahbub Ali, but when Mahbub arrives three days later, he refuses to help Kim escape. Mahbub Ali tells Colonel Creighton of Kim's ability to move between races, and Creighton recognises Kim's potential as a spy. Father Victor, who has just received the lama's payment for Kim's education, asks Creighton's advice. They decide that Kim should go to St Xavier's.

Commentary

Like the previous chapter, Chapter 6 is dominated by ideas of communication and understanding. Four letters are sent and received in the course of the chapter. The Colonel receives one telling him to mobilise, two are sent by the lama, and one by Kim. These last three are all written by an intermediary, and the lama's letters, reflecting thoughts in Tibetan, are dictated in the vernacular to the letter-writer, who translates them into a third language, English. This process inevitably obscures meaning. The most complete instance of misinterpretation is the lama's message to Father Victor. The Buddhist appeals to Almighty God to bless the celibate priest's 'succeedings to third an' fourth generation' (116).

Armed with the lama's letters and with Kim's documents, Father Victor asks Creighton to explain their meaning. Creighton correctly interprets the lama's intentions, but even he, an ethnographer, disclaims true understanding of the Indian people: 'The more one knows about natives the less can one say what they will or won't do' (124).

The cryptic discussion between Creighton and Mahbub Ali about Kim reopens the 'Great Game' plot. Between these two meaning and language are adapted to private ends. What is said is a metaphor for what is meant. While they seem to be talking of horses and of polo, they are really talking of Kim and of the 'game' of counter-espionage. Creighton deceives Father Victor for his own ends by pretending to despise Mahbub Ali, and by accounting for his interest in Kim as a scholarly one.

In this chapter, even Kim's powers of understanding are shown to be limited. He can see no meaning in the lines on the class-room board, and he assumes that the drummer-boy's talk of Liverpool is all lies. The dialogue of Mahbub Ali and Creighton angers him because he recognises that it reduces him to an object to be talked about and manipulated. Instinctively, however, Kim keeps his head and retains some superiority to Mahbub Ali by not revealing how much he already understands.

CHAPTER 7

Synopsis

Kim is told that he is to leave Umballa for St Xavier's. As he dictates a letter to the lama, he meets Creighton, who tests his discretion. Kim, aware of what is happening, pretends not to know the whereabouts of Creighton's house.

On the railway journey to Lucknow, Creighton tells Kim that he may have a future as a surveyor, indicating that a part of his work will be to gather intelligence. On arrival in Lucknow, Kim persuades his driver to give him a tour of the city. When he finally reaches St Xavier's, he finds the lama waiting at the gates. The lama says that he will see Kim occasionally, and they agree to correspond by letter.

The narrator describes the boys of St Xavier's. Born in all parts of India, they are used to hair-raising experiences. Kim's education, both formal and informal, progresses rapidly. He decides to avoid spending his holidays at a barrack school, and persuades a prostitute to dye his skin so that he can take to the Road once more. After a month of adventures, Kim once more meets Mahbub Ali near Umballa.

Commentary

The first chapters of *Kim* cover a brief span of time, less than a fortnight in all. By contrast, Chapter 7 covers four months, three of these coinciding with Kim's first term at St Xavier's. The narrator explains that his reader 'would scarcely be interested in Kim's experiences as a St Xavier's boy' (136). Instead, he gives an impressionistic account of the characteristic pupil and his background, before referring, even more sketchily, to Kim's growth in knowledge.

Four very different episodes make up the body of this 'bridge' chapter.

Kim's early conversations with Creighton are cryptic and cautious, verbal games to which both are temperamentally adapted. In total contrast is Kim's meeting with the lama at the gates of St Xavier's, when the boy tries to cling to the old man, passionately declaring his love. The lama responds with a deep affection, quite unlike Creighton's chilly curiosity.

The third episode is one of the novel's light-hearted, picaresque scenes. In the red-light district of Lucknow, Kim tells a young prostitute that, in his pursuit of a schoolmaster's 12-year-old daughter, he wants to dye his skin and pretend to be a gardener's boy. When he leaves, Kim enjoys a rich Indian meal, before entertaining a third-class railway compartment with his far-fetched tales. His strong sense of relief at escaping from British formality is forcefully conveyed.

Kim's own comment that he is a victim of circumstance 'as it might be a kick-ball' (131), follows up the message of the poem at the head of the chapter, which discusses the effect of the stars upon man. The chapter, with its movement from place to place, reflects Kim's struggle to maintain control of his own fate, and his limited success in so doing.

CHAPTER 8

Synopsis

Mahbub Ali instructs Kim to change his clothes, and he now appears as the Pathan's horse-boy. Mahbub Ali and Kim acknowledge that each holds the other's life in his hands. Kim tells Mahbub Ali of the search through Mahbub's possessions in the Kashmir Serai of Lahore, and reminds him of the delivery of the message to Creighton. He demands the freedom to wander through India in his school holidays.

Kim joins Mahbub Ali's retainers by their camp fire. He hears two men plotting to kill Mahbub Ali, and manages to warn him. Through Mahbub's skill, the would-be assassins are captured by the police.

Kim and Mahbub Ali, travel from Umballa to Simla with the train of horses. Mahbub Ali tells Kim that he is to spend the rest of his holidays at the home of a Simla antique dealer, Lurgan. Kim realises that Lurgan is another spy.

Commentary

Where the first four chapters develop Kim's relationship with one father-figure, the lama, Chapter 8 is taken up with his relationship to another, Mahbub Ali. The contrasts are striking. The lama is often distracted, withdrawn into his own world, but Mahbub Ali is as alert as Kim himself, and their dialogue takes the form of a battle of wits, each withholding information from the other. Where Kim provides food for the lama, usually by the exercise of his intelligence, the process is here reversed, as Mahbub Ali orders a meal for himself and his guest. The merchant and the city boy play at commerce together, with Kim offering news for money, giving it for love, but then accepting the money as a gift.

The episode in the railway yard, like that with the thieving priest in Chapter 3, is cast in the picaresque mode, as Kim and Mahbub Ali between them outwit their enemies and deliver them into the hands of the police.

The final section of the chapter is very different. Here the road up into the hills, and the town of Simla are described with the same richness of style as the Grand Trunk Road in Chapter 4. Simla, on its hillside, is a place of intrigue, a town of alleys and bolt-holes where secrets are kept and given away, an appropriate setting for the last words of the chapter, spoken by Mahbub Ali: 'Here begins the Great Game' (162).

CHAPTER 9

Synopsis

Kim is directed by a Hindu boy to the house of Lurgan, a restorer of pearls and turquoises, and a dealer in oriental antiquities and curiosities. Sleeping in the shop, among this alarming merchandise, Kim is awoken by a voice coming from a phonograph. Reminding himself that he is an Englishman, Kim breaks the wax cylinder in the darkness. Next day, Lurgan tries to mesmerise Kim into believing that a broken jug is whole. Kim holds out against the power of hypnotism by repeating the multiplication tables in English. Lurgan, who trains secret-service agents, realises that Kim has remarkable strength of will.

Kim's training begins in a series of memory tests, where the Hindu boy always surpasses him. During his ten days with Lurgan, Kim learns to disguise himself in many ways. When clients come into the shop, Lurgan makes Kim comment on them, and guess the real motive for their visit.

Four days before Kim leaves Simla, a Bengali, Hurree Chunder Mookerjee, arrives. He too belongs to the secret service. When Kim returns to school, they travel on the same tonga, and Mookerjee gives the boy a small case of medicine.

The narrator briefly describes Kim's schooldays, which come to an end when he is nearly 16. He also tells of the wanderings of the lama during this time. In the Jain temple at Benares, the lama tells a story which provides a commentary on his own relation to Kim. A defenceless calf is protected by an older elephant. When the calf reaches maturity, he proves to be Lord Buddha, and frees the older elephant from a crippling leg ring. The lama is startled to hear from the old soldier near Umballa that Kim has been to his home a few days before.

Commentary

In Chapter 9, Kim's special qualities are tested by Lurgan. We already know that Kim, in the words of the heading poem for the previous chapter, has 'two sides to his head', an Indian and a British side, and that his usefulness to the 'Great Game' lies in this combination. Lurgan is anxious to judge the balance between Kim's two sides, and it is significant that Kim surmounts the two psychological hurdles set by Lurgan by relying on his British education. In the dark night, he tells himself: 'I am a Sahib and the son of a Sahib and, which is twice as much more beside, a student of Nucklao' (165). Faced with the attempted hypnosis, he takes refuge in 'the multiplication-table in English!' (169).

The contrast between Kim and the Hindu boy extends this theme. In his murderous jealousy and fear of Kim, the boy tries to poison Lurgan. When Lurgan asks Kim what he would do in the Hindu boy's place, Kim carefully weighs up the alternatives, and decides that he would not try to kill Lurgan. If it were true that the intruder was preferred, he [Kim] would beat the intruder. In other words, Kim would try to find out the human truth before acting.

The well-trained Hindu boy easily surpasses Kim in the cerebral test of remembering the exact objects displayed on a tray, but Kim, whose insight and imagination are far greater, excels in the more speculative challenge of disguise and the analysis of motive. The introduction of Hurree Chunder Mookerjee, however, indicates the limits of Kim's imagination. ' "How comes it that this man is one of *us*?" thought Kim' (177). The human being, and in particular the secret service agent, is not always readily comprehensible. Hurree, as Kim is to discover later in the novel, is remarkably brave for a timid man. When he describes himself as a 'fearful' man, the ironic double meaning is not merely a joke at his own expense. Hurree is both frightened, and a powerful force to be reckoned with.

The final pages of the chapter reintroduce the lama, who has almost dropped out of sight. His progress through India, tracing the holy places, is by implication compared with Kim's wanderings in his school holidays. Both seek enlightenment, Kim from the variety of life, the lama from the exercise of prayer and worship. The brief sentences on Kim's progress at school, his reports, prize and performance in the cricket team, are placed in juxtaposition to his continuing love for the lama, to the lama's search, and to the inset story, told by the lama, of the Buddha and the elephant, with its message of salvation through love.

CHAPTER 10

Synopsis

Kim spends his school holidays with Mahbub Ali and Lurgan. With Mahbub Ali he travels to Bombay, Karachi and Quetta, and, in the following year, to Bikanir, Jeysalmir and to Jodhpur in Rajputan. At Christmas, he learns languages and other skills from Lurgan, in Simla.

Mahbub Ali and Lurgan persuade Creighton that Kim should leave St Xavier's at 16, and travel for six months with the lama. Mahbub takes Kim to Huneefa, a sorceress, who puts magic charms upon him, and dyes his skin. From Hurree Babu Kim receives the turquoise amulet of a member of the secret service. He is now one of the sons of the charm.

Commentary

Chapter 10, like the previous chapter, explores ideas of learning and experience. Here it is Mahbub Ali and Hurree Babu, rather than St Xavier's and Lurgan, who attempt to impart wisdom to Kim. The vacation journeys with Mahbub Ali are described in a brief allusive style, marked by a frequent use of the dash as a form of punctuation. The manner of the account implies that much is left untold, that the narrator has chosen suggestion rather than detail. He tells us that, on the way to the mysterious city of Bikanir, Kim 'nearly died of thirst' (186), but he tells us no more.

The opening poem, from an unfinished play by Kipling, gives a very precise analogue for the conflict of opinion over Kim's future which develops between Mahbub Ali and Lurgan on the one side, and Creighton on the other. Mahbub and Lurgan argue that Kim, like a hawk which has been captured in the wild, cannot be kept in partial freedom for too long, but must be put to the task at once. In the early part of the chapter, Kim is seen from the outside rather than from within. He is absent during this significant conversation about him, and the reader only re-enters Kim's consciousness when Hurree Babu gives him the amulet and tells him about the fellowship of the charm.

The passage with Huneefa is one of those in which Kipling hints at a darker side to Indian life. He said himself that it was the only part of the novel that he had researched in the India Office Library. This spell-casting is Mahbub Ali's gift to Kim. Even Hurree Babu, an official freethinker, is made very uneasy by the ritual. He, in his turn, gives Kim a gift, the turquoise amulet, an introduction to another closed world, that of the secret service. Magic is presented to the reader with caution. It is never asserted that Huneefa's charms have any effect upon Kim, and even Mahbub Ali sees it as an insurance rather than a certainty.

CHAPTER 11

Synopsis

In the railway station at Lucknow, Kim experiences a state of depression and loses his sense of identity. He talks with a Hindu holy man who recognises Kim's state of mind. On arrival in

Benares, a Jat (northern) farmer asks Kim for help with his sick son. Kim meets the lama again in the Jain temple and gives the Jat medicine. Overjoyed at Kim's return, the lama tells him that the quest for the river cannot be completed without him. In the early morning, the grateful Jat returns. The quinine has cured the boy's fever, and, in his gratitude, the father gives Kim and the lama food for the journey.

They leave together on a train from Benares to Delhi. At Sumna Road, a secret service man, E23, disguised as a Mahratta (a Hindu from the south-west), gets into the carriage. He and Kim exchange signs, and E23 explains that he is in danger of his life. Kim disguises him as a Saddhu (a holy man). The train arrives in Delhi.

Commentary

The train journey, with the transforming of E23, is part of the adventure plot of the novel, but the lama's presence in the carriage provides a reproving commentary on Kim's pride on his own achievements, both here, and in the earlier episode of the healing of the Jat's child. Kim is using skills learnt from Lurgan and Hurree Babu, skills taught to him for secret-service ends, but the trusting lama assumes that Kim's intention is either religious or humanitarian.

A further complication to the adventure plot is provided by Kipling's introduction of the hot-tempered Jat. The love of father for son is one of the themes of *Kim*, and the Jat's desperate desire to save his boy, and his gratitude to Kim, help him to resist the forces of anger and jealousy, and submit himself to Kim's control. The Jat's anger that Kim should devote attention to E23 is both a contrast to this and a parallel with the gentle but uneasy bewilderment of the lama. The apparent simplicity of the joyful reunion of Kim and the lama in the temple is immediately complicated by the cross-currents of such external demands upon Kim.

CHAPTER 12

Synopsis

At Delhi railway station, a young policeman searches the train, but fails to recognise E23. Leaving the train, E23 insults another policeman, who proves to be a fellow-member of the secret service, Strickland. Having delivered his message, E23 disappears, and Kim and the lama continue their journey by train to Saharunpore. They walk in the countryside for several days, before a message from the Ranee summons them to her house. Kim finds Hurree Babu there, playing the part of a travelling doctor. Hurree tells him that a Russian spy and his French companion are intriguing with two kings from the northern states. He is on his way to investigate, and persuades Kim to take the lama into the hills on the same track.

Commentary

Kim and the lama return to their interrupted quest for the lama's river. In the three years since their first journey Kim has almost grown into a man, and his relationship with the lama has deepened with his increasing maturity. The divisions within Kim, however, have complicated that relationship. At Saharunpore, the lama thankfully shakes off the noise and discomfort of their journey, not recognising that the incident with E23 is a part of Kim's new life. Kim's double role leads him to encourage the lama to climb higher, salving his conscience by telling himself that this is what the lama wants to do. For all the lama's innocent profundity, he fails to understand Kim's motives. Seen through the perspective of the lama's philosophy, Kim's adventures are no more than a worldly illusion.

The account of the lama's attitude to the Ranee is often humorous. On arrival at Saharunpore, the lama leads Kim on a circular walk, intended temporarily to evade the Ranee. Unable to resist her entreaties, the lama (to Kim's wry amusement) is faced with more demands for holy charms. As they leave for the hills, with Kim bowed down by her gifts, the two laugh together at the absurd idea that the Ranee will eventually escape from the treadmill of worldly vanities and become a Buddhist nun. Even the lama, with his infinite optimism, finds it hard to conceive of such a possibility.

CHAPTER 13

Synopsis

As Kim and the lama walk up into the mountains, the lama rejoices in the return to his natural habitat. Hurree Babu, searching for the Russian and his companion, crosses their path from time to time. When he finds the spies, Hurree joins their party, pretending to be the emissary of a local rajah.

Hurree and the two spies come upon the lama instructing Kim from his own drawing of the Buddhist wheel of life. The Russian first attempts to buy, and then snatches and tears the drawing. He strikes the lama, outraging the religious tabus of the local baggage-carriers. Kim violently attacks and injures the Russian and both the Frenchman and Kim fire their guns. The carriers rescue the lama and run away towards Shamlegh, taking the spies' luggage. Hurree Babu remains with the spies, telling them that they are in danger of being executed for sacrilege.

Commentary

The first part of the chapter contains some of the finest descriptive writing in the novel, as the lama and Kim travel into the mountains. Here the balance between them alters. The lama seems to become younger and walks with greater ease, while Kim, unused to the terrain, limps and labours uphill. He, like Hurree Babu, prefers to stick to the road, while the lama takes short cuts over seemingly impenetrable hillsides. Kim and the Babu follow a secular path, but the lama's mental freedom allows him to proceed confidently into the unknown.

Structurally, the chapter stresses this contrast. Passages describing Kim and the lama alone are interspersed with encounters with Hurree Babu. After the climactic episode, the groups separate once more, Kim taking the lama to Shamlegh, high in the mountains, and Hurree making his way to the British summer capital of Simla with the spies.

Kim's duplicity in waiting for Hurree and the spies to come upon the lama and himself leads to the conflict, and to the lama's illness. The whole chapter presents a disturbing tension between the lama's innocent pleasure in the return to the mountains and the devious behaviour of the more knowing Kim. The drawn wheel of life from which the lama seeks to enlighten Kim, becomes – in this chapter and the next – a symbol of the issues raised. The lama is warning Kim against greed when the Russian tries to snatch the paper from him.

CHAPTER 14

Synopsis

Kim and the lama reach the mountain village of Shamlegh. The lama spends the night in anguished meditation upon the evils of aggression. In the morning, Kim is given the red kilta containing the spies' papers and instruments. He keeps the incriminating documents, and throws the rest 2000 feet down the mountain side. The Woman of Shamlegh carries a message to Hurree Babu, who replies telling Kim to go back to the plains. The lama has also decided to return, believing that he has done wrong in coming into the hills. The Woman of Shamlegh, attracted by Kim, begs him to remain, but he insists upon leaving. On her orders, the Woman's many husbands carry the lama in a litter.

Commentary

After the drama of Chapter 13, Chapter 14 is largely reflective in tone. Once again, a spiritual call to the lama, his guilt at a display of anger, coincides with the earthly call of Kim. Both have to return to the plain of India. The counterpoint between Kim's two vocations, as chela and secret-service man, continues here, for while the lama wrestles with his soul, and unhappily contemplates the anger of Kim himself, Kim sorts through the spies' papers and is tempted to keep their geometrical equipment. He puts it from him, as the lama must put away the hills. The rejected articles smash upon the mountain side, and Kim silences his regret for their loss, by recalling that 'a Sahib cannot very well steal' (275). His attitude to plunder contrasts with that of the hill-men, who rapidly consume and absorb the Russian's property.

The temptation offered by the Woman of Shamlegh is presented more obliquely. It is appropriate that she, whom Kim recognises as the first women to treat him as a man, should also be the only character to guess at his true nationality. He confirms her guess by kissing her and by shaking her hand. If the attack on the Frenchman represents one kind of maturity for Kim, his conversations with the Woman represent a real sexual dialogue, not the casual erotic invitations to which he has been subjected before.

CHAPTER 15

Synopsis

Hurree Babu escorts the spies to Simla, making sure that their discomfiture is witnessed by as many people as possible.

After a slow journey, Kim and the lama arrive at the house of the Ranee. Kim collapses from exhaustion and is nursed back to health. After his illness, he hears that the lama has fallen into a stream, but fails to understand that this was the long-sought river of enlightenment.

To Kim's relief, Hurree takes away the papers. As Kim lies asleep on the earth, the lama and Mahbub Ali talk warmly together. When he wakes, the lama tells him that he has torn himself away from nirvana in order to ensure the salvation of Kim.

Commentary

The ending of the book brings resolution of its main themes. Kim calls the Ranee 'mother', and Mahbub Ali recognises that he and the lama, for all their differences, have both been fathers to Kim. The lama finds his river, but understands that his love for Kim means more than nirvana.

When Kim lies on the earth, the narrator tells us that it carries the seeds of grain, but, unlike grass, is eternal. The earth is symbolic of Kim's attachment to India itself, as well as of his youth and potential power. Before he sleeps, he revolves in his mind the words: 'I am Kim. I am Kim. And what is Kim?' (305). The positive statements of identity are followed by a question about the nature of that identity. Having followed Kim to the threshold of manhood, we are still in doubt about his future, and the novel ends without resolving the uncertainty.

3 THEMES, ISSUES AND BACKGROUND

3.1 INDIA IN THE LATER NINETEENTH CENTURY

Before the passing of the India Act of 1858, responsibility for the administration of India was in the hands of the East India Company. The final transfer of power from the company to the British Crown was a direct result of the Indian Mutiny of 1857–8, a revolt, originating in the Bengal army, which spread to large parts of upper and central India. British soldiers and their families were cut off in Cawnpore and Lucknow, and those who surrendered at Cawnpore were massacred. Lucknow was relieved by General Havelock in the autumn of 1857, Delhi was taken in September, and peace was proclaimed in July 1858. Reprisals were carried out with considerable ferocity.

These events had already assumed the status of myth during Kipling's time in India, and it is natural that he should introduce recollections of them into *Kim*. In Chapter 3, the old soldier, the Rissaldar, recalls his own part in the mutiny, as a native officer who remained loyal to the British. His account of riding seventy miles with an Englishwoman and her child; his sense of having been 'an outcast among my own kin' (63); and his pride in his medals and his sword, these must have been recognisable elements of many tales of the 'black year'.

The popular hero of the mutiny was John Nicholson, who died at the recapture of Delhi at the early age of 36. 'Nikal Seyn' had already acquired an heroic aura before the mutiny. After his death a Punjabi ballad circulated, telling the story of his last battle in elevated terms. This is the 'old song' which the Rissaldar sings to

Kim and the lama (66). It is significant, however, that Kim's guide to Lucknow, an Indian 'told Kim many astounding things where an English guide would have talked of the Mutiny' (133). For an Indian, Lucknow is a Mogul (Moslem) city, whose history goes back far beyond the mutiny. Simla, by contrast, was a new British creation, and, in the novel, Mahbub Ali's uncle could recall a time when there were only two houses there.

The insecurity and resentment engendered by the mutiny were slow to die, and led to a greater rigidity in Anglo-Indian relations. The building of railways and the extension of the Grand Trunk Road to the north helped to bring the subcontinent more firmly under central control. In the course of their travels, Kim and the lama make extensive use of both road and railway, and the lama gradually becomes familiar with what Kim calls the 'te-rain'.

In Kipling's own day, Indian politics were dominated by the threat of Russian infiltration into the north. Behind the dangerous North West Frontier was Afghanistan, where the Amirs held an increasingly pro-Russian stance. The murder of the British legation in Kabul led to the Second Afghan War of 1878–80, and *Kim*, the events of which take place between 1878 and 1881, reflects the nervousness and uncertainty of a time when the loyalty of the northern rulers was continuously in question.

Five kings, and those of Hilás and Bunár in particular, are suspected of entering negotiations with Russia. Hilás and Bunár were not the names of Indian states, but they have been tentatively identified with the northern provinces, Chilas and Buner.

The first message which Kim carries for Mahbub Ali warns of impending insurrection. This is avoided by swift and decisive action. The action is not sufficiently punitive, however, and further trouble is allowed to ferment. The papers which Kim carries down from the hills at the end of the novel contain proof that either Hilás or Bunár is intriguing with the Russians, and that a plan exists to sweep into northern India down the newly built British roads. The Russian and the Frenchman have been surveying for this purpose.

The Russian war never came. Kipling lived to see Afghanistan gain independence, but died before India and Pakistan became independent nations in 1947. Lahore, the city where the novel *Kim* opens, is now in Pakistan.

3.2 THE GEOGRAPHY OF *KIM*

A reader of *Kim* needs to study the map of India in order to understand the movements of its characters. Kim travels in north-western India with Mahbub Ali, and the lama worships at Buddhist shrines throughout India and Ceylon [Sri Lanka], but the main events of the novel take place in the central northern state of Punjab and in north-eastern India. The 'Great Game' of espionage is being played, not on the North West Frontier, but on the eastern border in the foothills of the Himalayas and Karakorums.

In one of Kipling's finest stories, 'The Man who would be King' (1890), two ne'er do wells make their way into the north-western kingdom of Kafiristan. The terrible end to the story is evidence of the menace of the country beyond the north-western border. By contrast, *Kim*'s north-eastern hills are presented idealistically, rising out of the dirt and noise of the Indian plain. Beyond the north-eastern border lies, not the bandit country of the Khyber pass, but the mountains of Tibet, whence comes the most perfectly good of all Kipling's characters, the lama.

3.3 RACIAL DIVISION

Ideas of conflict and difference are central to any reading of *Kim*. The whole structure of the novel is built up on patterns of contrast, which are intricately interwoven with the plot. The final message of *Kim*, however, is not one of disharmony, but of synthesis and communication.

The behaviour of the British in India is a recurring subject in Kipling's early work. He sharply contrasts their way of life (which often continues in defiance of landscape and climate) with that of the native Indians.

In *Kim*, the narrator frequently draws the attention of the reader to features of Indian life which differ from those in Britain. Kipling explores this theme chiefly through the character of Kim, the British boy who has acquired Indian qualities, and who constantly tests these against those which he learns at school. Kim uses a twig as a toothbrush, sits cross-legged without strain, and falls asleep whenever he finds something boring. Unlike British boys, he regards prostitutes as a natural part of life. After his abrupt transfer to a British barracks, Kim feels revulsion at eating his 'unappetising' meals in company with others. He prefers 'to turn his back on the world at meals' (118). But, if Europeans eat together, they separate afterwards, and Kim finds life as a Sahib lonely. His 'solitary passage' (131) in a second-class compartment depresses him: 'this strong loneliness among white men preyed on him' (115).

'For his own ends or Mahbub's business, Kim could lie like an Oriental', comments the narrator, who has just noted that 'Kim was the one soul in the world who had never told him [Mahbub] a lie' (30). Mahbub himself would distrust a totally honest person, and warns Kim of the dangers of telling the truth. Indiscriminate truth-telling is another characteristic associated with the Sahib, and one which Kim regards with a certain scorn. 'The English do eternally tell the truth' (155), he thinks, and turns that quality to his own advantage. Yet this same exceptional quality attracts Kim to the lama: 'Kim . . . knew that the old man was speaking the truth, which is a thing a native on the road seldom presents to a stranger' (23).

British and Indian attitudes to time are also the subject of numerous comments by the narrator. 'The easy, uncounted Eastern minutes slid by' (205), or 'Swiftly – as Orientals understand speed – with long explanations, with abuse and windy talk, carelessly, amid a hundred checks for little things forgotten, the untidy camp broke up' (157) are characteristic references to this fundamental difference in approach.

Through the narrator, Kipling is careful to distinguish what he calls the 'native born', those born in India, from the British settlers who have come from Europe to India. Kim, like Kipling, is native-born, and scorns the others as outsiders. At school, Kim 'learned to wash himself with the Levitical scrupulosity of the native-born, who in his heart considers the Englishman rather dirty' (137). He is careful not to say too much about his own life 'for St Xavier's looks down on boys who "go native all-together" ' (138).

There is little description of conventional life in British India. Kim's acquaintance with young Englishmen revolves around 'intrigue' in Lahore, and this is also the way of life in Simla. We have a brief glimpse of the shooting habits of the officers on leave, of a dinner party given by Colonel Creighton and his wife for the Commander-in-Chief in Umballa, and a fuller picture of the men and wives of the Maverick regiment. Elsewhere we encounter British policemen, most of whom are secret-service men in disguise.

By contrast, Kipling presents a variety of different Indian homes and families. There are the old soldier with his three sons, and the Ranee with, just off-stage, her daughter, long suffering son-in-law, and grandsons; the hot-tempered Jat with his baby son, the cultivator's wife talking of her husband's second cousin, even the child who wanders in from the village to play with the lama's rosary – each of these minor figures reinforces a sense that India is a land of kinship.

Kipling makes considerable use of railway scenes to point up the contrast between the two cultures. Much of Chapter 2 describes Kim's journey with the lama from Lahore to Umballa, with an account of the conversation in the overcrowded carriage, and of the kindness shown to Kim and the lama by the prostitute and the cultivator's wife. In strict contrast to this is Kim's journey from Umballa to Lucknow, in 'an empty second-class next to Colonel Creighton's first . . . This solitary passage was very different from that joyful down-journey in the third-class with the lama. "Sahibs get little pleasure of travel", he reflected' (130–1). Leaving Lucknow at the end of term, Kim decides to leave his luggage behind and to disguise himself: 'Sahibs are always tied to their baggage' (139). Returned to his Indian self, he watches a fellow-schoolboy, uncomfortably over-dressed in the heat, climb into a second-class compartment, while he himself happily becomes the 'life and soul' of a third (141).

In brief, one central theme of *Kim* is the contrast between the emotional warmth and imaginative power of India, and the discipline and reserve of the British. Kim's passage between the two loosely parallels Kipling's own, and suggests to the discerning reader that the author shares more with his hero than the letter K and an early departure from school.

3.4 RELIGIOUS DIVISION

(i) Buddhism

A number of writers have expressed surprise that, through the person of the lama, Kipling should exalt Buddhism over other more widespread and active religions of India.

Kipling first encountered Buddhism at school when he read *The Light of Asia*, published in 1879 by Sir Edwin Arnold (1832–1904). Arnold's poetic account of the life of Buddha became a cult work in late Victorian England. The original founder of the religion, Siddhartha Gautama, or the Buddha, probably lived between 563 and 483 BC. The surviving accounts of the Buddha's life are mingled with legend, but certain central events are documented, and marked by Buddhist shrines. Among these are the four holy places to which Kim's lama travels: the birthplace at Kapilavastu; Bodh Gaya, where the Buddha received enlightenment; the deer park at Sarnath, where he preached his first sermon; and Kusingara, where the Buddha died.

The river for which the lama is searching will ensure his enlightenment. For the Buddhist enlightenment is a form of salvation, 'nirvana'. Those who achieve nirvana escape from the cycle of rebirth, to which all others are subject. Buddhism teaches a clear lesson of cause and effect. A life devoted to worldly, greedy desires will result in rebirth in a lower form of life. When the lama speaks of men and women as 'caught up in the wheel', he means that they cannot detach themselves from earthly things, and so must await the next turn of the sequence. As a general rule only ascetics can hope to find nirvana, but laymen and women can acquire merit by various acts. In *Kim* it is usually the women characters who are said to acquire merit – the prostitute on the train, the Ranee and the Woman of Shamlegh. All are noticeably worldly, and there is some humour in the lama's innocent approach to their 'virtue'. He allows the Ranee to acquire merit by feeding and sustaining him, but he always ends by giving her a charm to secure more grandchildren for her.

Buddhism teaches the suppression of worldly desires, and of the individual ego. In its purest form it requires complete withdrawal from the things of this world. In the company of Kim, the lama rarely achieves this. On the Grand Trunk Road he seems to abstract himself and pray over his rosary, while Kim is entranced by the sights around him, but he later confesses to a delight in 'the new people upon the roads' (104). The lama often finds himself caught up in the human at the expense of the superhuman. In an unguarded moment, he amuses a small child with his rosary, or, in a moment of anger, he nearly hits the Russian who has attacked him. As the former head of an influential Tibetan monastery, which he has left to go on pilgrimage, the lama occasionally finds it hard to humble himself. Most important of all, he becomes deeply attached to Kim. The lama tries to explain this to himself in terms of his search for the river. He is convinced that he will only find it through the agency of Kim, and feels no anxiety or impatience as a result. In the event, when on the point of nirvana, the lama turns back to take Kim with him. Earthly attachment triumphs over spiritual salvation. One precursor of the lama's act is Christ, another the semi-Christian Buddha whom Kipling knew from *The Light of Asia*.

(ii) Christianity

Both Buddhism and Christianity were inspired by the life of a great master, who, in the case of Jesus Christ, is also considered to be divine. Deriving as it does from Judaism, Christianity posits the existence of God, the creator, where, for Buddhists, there is no all-powerful god.

The two faiths, however, have much in common. The doctrines of Christ insist upon a moral code of unselfish living as both a proof of salvation and a means of achieving it. Yet many Christian saints and monastics have been less concerned with the reform of the world than with the mystic flight of the soul into union with God. The path of mysticism and the pursuit of spiritual self-annihilation is practised widely among Buddhists, but unselfish behaviour and giving, 'acquiring merit', if seen as a lower path towards enlightenment, are still of importance in the Buddhist philosophy.

If Buddhism differs from Christianity in believing that all creation is involved in a cycle of rebirth, its assertion that a virtuous life leads to a higher form, and a worldly and sinful one to a lower existence, is obviously comparable with the Christian belief in an ultimate judgement resulting in salvation or damnation. Like all Eastern religions, however, Buddhism is less concerned with the individual ego than is Christianity, and, as Kipling makes clear in *Kim*, social divisions, and even differences between man and the animal kingdom, are far more blurred and indistinct for the Buddhist than for the Christian.

Christianity as such features rarely in Kipling's writing. An exception is the short story, 'The Gardener' (1926), where a Christ-like figure appears in a First World War cemetery. In the huge and alarming context of India, and of *Kim*, Christianity is presented as small-minded and inadequate, a view which was reiterated by a later novelist, E. M. Forster (1879–1970), in *A Passage to India* (1924). It is the lama who represents the ideal against which that inadequacy is tested.

In Chapter 5, Kim is captured by the Anglican chaplain of the Mavericks, Arthur Bennett. Together with the Roman Catholic priest, Father Victor, he tries to decide what should be done with the boy. The lama is called in, and the four conduct a dialogue constrained by language and prejudice. Bennett is unwilling and unable to address the lama directly: 'Bennett looked at him with the triple-ringed uninterest of the creed that lumps nine-tenths of the world under the title of "heathen" ' (99).

Roman Catholic priests generally come off better than Anglican clergy in Kipling's Indian stories. Father Victor is less prejudiced and more humane than Bennett. Bennett recognises this pragmatically, although he draws no conclusions from it:

> Between himself and the Roman Catholic Chaplain of the Irish contingent lay, as Bennett believed, an unbridgeable gulf, but it was noticeable that whenever the Church of England dealt with a human problem she was very likely to call in the Church of Rome. Bennett's official abhorrence of the Scarlet Woman and all her ways was only equalled by his private respect for Father Victor (96).

Bennett, a stereotyped and one dimensional character, comes close to being the villain of *Kim*. His limiting racial prejudices make him automatically condemn Kim as a thief until he realises that the boy is white.

In the discussion between the churchmen, Kipling uses linguistic misunderstanding to highlight spiritual division. Only Kim can interpret all that is said. His version of what takes place, however, is subtly refracted by his own attitude and understanding. The boy experiences irritation as he tries to translate the lama's quest for the river from 'the vernacular to the clumsy English' (101). By implication English is a language inappropriate for his description of spiritual matters. Father Victor recognising the gap in his own perception, comments: 'I'd give a good deal to be able to talk the vernacular. A river that washes away sin!', where Bennett's comment is 'But this is gross blasphemy!' (101).

The irony lies, not just in problems of linguistics, but in Bennett's failure to see that Christianity and Buddhism have an important symbol in common. There is a clear literary relationship between *Kim* and John Bunyan's *Pilgrim's Progress* (1678), where the Christian pilgrims must cross the river in order to enter eternal life. The lama's river is also the path to eternity, and approximates, even more closely than Bunyan's, to the river of life, flowing from the throne of the Lamb, which forms part of the vision of the final book of the Bible, *The Revelation*.

(iii) Other forms of belief

Mahbub Ali, the Pathan horse-dealer, is the chief representative of Mohammedanism in *Kim*. A sceptic by nature, Mahbub Ali is still instinctively and superstitiously controlled by Islamic beliefs, and his language is scattered with references both to Allah and to the devils of his faith. To him, the lama is an idolator, and Kim an unbeliever. When Mahbub Ali pays Huneefa, a witch-woman, to give Kim supernatural protection, he excuses himself by saying: 'I am a *Sufi* [free-thinker], but when one can get blindsides of a woman, a stallion, or a devil, why go round to invite a kick?' (197).

Buddhism, Mohammedanism and Christianity are clearly distinguished in *Kim*. Disentangling other religious groups is less easy. Hinduism, the dominant Indian religion, is comparatively little discussed, though the caste system is emphasised. This religious and social hierarchy dominates Indian life then as now. There is ample evidence of the rigidity of the system in the novel. On the Grand Trunk Road, Kim sees a party of Sansis, gypsies, 'all other castes gave them ample room; for the Sansi is deep pollution' (71). The next passer-by is a Sikh devotee, an Akali, a type whom Kim immediately recognises and avoids. On the train to Umballa, a Ludhiana Sikh irritates a Dogra soldier 'for a Dogra is of other caste than a Sikh' (37). Kim insults a Sweeper, a member of one of the lowest castes, by calling him an Od, a casteless one. The lama lives in the temple of the Jains, a sect who go to great lengths to avoid killing any form of animal life, however small.

The most significant contribution of Hinduism to the novel comes in Chapter 11, where Kim, in a moment of depression, meets an aged holy man, a bairagi, who recognises Kim's state of mind, and wishes him well: ' "Go in hope, little brother", he said. "It is a long road to the feet of the One; but thither do we all travel." Kim did not feel so lonely after this' (203).

Hurree Chunder Mookerjee, a Bengali, describes himself as a follower of the philosopher Herbert Spencer (1820–1903). Spencer's belief that phenomena have a materialistic rather than a supernatural explanation had considerable influence among educated Indians in the nineteenth century. Hurree Babu, however, is not totally confident in his unbelief, and his references to Spencer in the novel are as much indications of the 'fearfulness' which he is trying to combat, as of a fixed philosophical standpoint. He tells Mahbub Ali: 'It is an awful thing still to dread the magic that you contemptuously investigate – to collect folk-lore for the Royal Society with a lively belief in all Powers of Darkness' (197). Hurree Babu and Creighton both have an ambition to become Fellows of the Royal Society, the highest honour for a British scientist.

Kim's religion is even more uncertain than his racial affinity. In his open-minded state, he rapidly identifies the Virgin Mary with the Mohammedan Bibi Miriam, and simply adds 'an entirely new set of Gods and Godlings' (130) to the ones he knows already. In one of his moments of doubt he asks Mahbub Ali: 'What am I? Mussalman, Hindu, Jain or Buddhist? That is a hard knot.' He gets the reply:

Thou art beyond question an unbeliever, and therefore thou wilt be damned. So says my Law – or I think it does. But thou art also my Little Friend of all the World, and I love thee. So says my heart. This matter of creeds is like horseflesh. The wise man knows horses are good – that there is a profit to be made from all; and for myself – but that I am a good *Sunni* and hate the men of Tirah – I could believe the same of all the Faiths . . . the Faiths are like the horses. Each has merit in its own country (158).

Mahbub's use of the word 'merit', a word associated with the lama, reminds us of the novel's pairing of these two 'good' fathers to Kim. Mahbub's understanding of the relativity of faith is appropriate to the man, expressed at length, and through the metaphors of his own calling. The lama, hearing Kim refer to the Arian farmer as 'low-caste', puts the same point in an equally characteristic manner, pithy and reproving: 'Low-caste I did not say, for how can that be which is not?' (52).

3.5 DRESS

In his account of a multiracial society, Kipling stresses the importance of dress as a means of identification. Dress reveals caste, and so establishes the hierarchy and the mode of communication. When the hill-men in the Ranee's train see the lama's red tam o'shanter hat, their attitude to him changes abruptly. Even the colour of the lama's hat would tell the well-informed that he is from western Tibet. Mahbub Ali's gorgeous clothes are an immediate indication both of his character and his religion.

In his chameleon-like progress, Kim varies his dress, and even on occasion his skin colour, throughout the book. At the opening his foster-mother makes him dress as a European, but, when 'intrigue' demands, he changes into a low-caste Hindu costume. For his second journey with the lama, the secret service give him a complete 'chela' outfit, supplied by Lurgan, in whose house Kim has learnt the arts of disguise: 'The shop was full of all manner of dresses and turbans, and Kim was apparelled variously as a young Mohammedan of good family, an oilman, and once – which was a joyous evening – as the son of an Oudh landholder in the fullest of full dress' (174).

The most significant of the metamorphoses are those in which Kim crosses the barrier between white man and Indian. The transformation into a sahib is an uncomfortable one because sahib dress is inappropriate to the climate. 'Kim, newly washed all over, in a horrible stuff that rasped his arms and legs' (108). Kim 'squatted as only the natives can – in spite of the abominable clinging trousers' (113). When, at the end of term, Kim changes both his colour and his clothes, he is once more suited to his surroundings. Changing back is more difficult. The colour is not easily washed off, and Kim goes to Lurgan's house as a Eurasian, half-Indian, half-European, 'in badly fitting shop-clothes' (162).

Kim's disguises figure prominently in the adventure plot. At a more profound level, his changes of role contribute to his identity crisis. 'Who is Kim?' he asks, and the answer could be, a Hindu, a Buddhist neophyte, a British schoolboy, a spy, a Eurasian, according to circumstance. Yet, in religious terms, such role changes can seem superficial. Kim's repetition of his own name, 'I am Kim – Kim – Kim' (244) is like a meditational prayer, where the repeated word, the mantra, is the means to the mystic flight of the soul. That the lama's life of prayer is intended to negate personal identity, suggests yet another way of approaching the book's central theme of division and wholeness.

3.6 SPOKEN LANGUAGE

The orientalist and linguist, Alexander Hamilton (1762–1824) declared that: 'One great misfortune that attends us European travellers in India is, the want of knowledge of their languages, and they being so numerous, that "one entire century could be too short a time to learn them all" '. Hamilton himself taught Indian languages at Haileybury, a school which trained Indian civil servants, and the parent establishment of Kipling's own school at Westward Ho! Even in Kipling's day, few Europeans were at all fluent in any of the Indian tongues, and the barrier to communication was an important factor in determining the relationship of Indians and British.

The discussion of language differences in *Kim* is both extensive and complex, creating a psychological and social network which illustrates many of the themes of the novel. On the simplest level, *Kim* is remarkable for its ability to suggest movement among a variety of languages while using only one, English. A few words in other tongues are scattered through the book, to considerable effect, but they represent a tiny proportion of the whole text.

The major languages of *Kim* are English, Hindustani, and the Moslem tongue, Urdu. The British referred to these two native languages of northern India as the 'vernacular' or common speech, and Kipling too uses the expression. Several other languages are also mentioned, helping to build up an impression of linguistic complexity. The lama finds monks in Ceylon speaking Pali, the ancient Buddhist language, and uses 'ornate Chinese' (213) in bidding farewell to the Jain temple. Some of the visitors to Lurgan's shop speak Bengali, and the people of Shamlegh use a mountain dialect of their own. The Russian spy and his French companion communicate in French (French being the language of polite speech in Russia at this date) and Hurree Babu finds that, although he learnt his French in Chandernagore, he cannot follow their dialogue: ' "Now what the deuce is good of Chandernagore being so close to Calcutta and all", said Hurree . . . "if I cannot understand their French? They talk so par*t*icularly fast!" ' (258).

A knowledge of languages is a key to understanding. Where Bennett and Father Victor cannot distinguish the lama from any other wandering holy man, Creighton who studies ethnography and speaks the vernacular fluently, is at once aware of the old man's status. In the same way, Kim, who moves with ease between English and the vernacular, is aware of Creighton's special quality when he hears him talk in 'fluent and picturesque Urdu . . . No man could be a fool who knew the language so intimately' (131). When he hears Lurgan speak, Kim again draws his own conclusions: 'the accent of his Urdu, the intonation of his English, showed that he was anything but a Sahib' (166–7).

The knowledge of languages is one essential qualification for the Indian secret service, and Kipling stresses the way in which this knowledge sets the players of the Great Game apart from the rank and file. Once dressed as a sahib, it is assumed that Kim, like the drummer boy, will not realise that he is being insulted or cheated. Only his special linguistic knowledge protects him from exploitation. Mahbub Ali sells horses to young officers who, 'through sheer ignorance of the vernacular, grossly' insult him (157). India, Kipling implies, can only be penetrated by those who understand the language.

Even English, the language in which the novel is written, is capable of displaying difference. At the outset, Kim's English is distinguished as Eurasian, an effect which Kipling achieves by distinctive spelling of a few words, and by a special kind of sentence structure. Here Kim is speaking to the regimental priests about the lama:

> 'When he takes those beads like that, you see, he always wants to be quiett . . . He says he is very sorree that he cannot find the River now any more. He says, Why have you no disciples, and stop bothering him?' (102–4).

Here, Kipling is not only giving us an impression of Kim's imperfect English, but also reminding us of the dangers of translation. This was not what the lama said, Kim is reinterpreting it in his own terms.

Hurree Babu's English is a more extreme version of Kim's Eurasian dialect. In his conversation with Kim toward the end of Chapter 12, the Babu shifts more than once between English and the vernacular. His English is pompous, introducing mispronounced long words, and, as with many Indian speakers, leaving out the definite article: 'Of course, I tell you this unoffeecially to elucidate political situation' (241). On occasion, Kim asks Hurree Babu to speak in the vernacular, which he finds easier to understand than his elaborate English. The Babu's vernacular is presented to the reader in straightforward English, without special spelling. However, his vernacular has a marked biblical flavour, accentuated by the frequent use of 'thee' and 'thou'. Modern English has no intimate 'you' form, and the archaism serves this purpose well.

Kipling's presentation of 'Indian' English has, of course, a humorous side, but the prominence of language as an issue in *Kim* serves a serious purpose. At the heading of Chapter 8, Kipling places two verses of his own poem about 'The Two-Sided Man':

> Something I owe to the soil that grew –
> More to the life that fed –
> But most to Allah Who gave me two
> Separate sides to my head.
>
> I should go without shirts or shoes
> Friends, tobacco or bread
> Sooner than for an instant lose
> Either side of my head (145).

The two sides of Kim's head are the English and the Indian, and these are reflected in language. After entering St Xavier's, Kim begins to divide his thoughts into those in English and those in the vernacular. It is usually assumed that Kim's 'vernacular' is Hindustani, but it is clear that he converses in Urdu with both Creighton and the lama. Emotional or relaxed thoughts are in the vernacular; active, rational and practical thoughts in English. Sitting on the steps of the Jain temple, longing for roast beef (the cow is sacred to Hindus and certainly never eaten in a Jain temple), Kim 'swore to himself in the language of St Xavier's' (213). After the Frenchman has fired at him ' "By Jove!" Kim was thinking hard in English. "This is dam' tight place, but *I* think it is self-defence" ' (263).

Such sentiments are inappropriate in the context of Kim's peaceful travels with the lama: 'Each long, perfect day rose behind Kim for a barrier to cut him off from his race and his mother-tongue. He slipped back to thinking and dreaming in the vernacular' (232). The same distinctions are evident when Kim is disturbed by the sexual approaches of the woman of Shamlegh. He has been worrying about the security of the spies' letters, evidently an English anxiety, but now a new note enters, calling for another mental language: 'This time Kim thought in the vernacular as he waxed down the oilskin edges of the packets' (278).

3.7 WRITTEN LANGUAGE

Written language can also create misunderstanding. The letters exchanged between Father Victor and the lama mystify both, because the process of translation and transliteration has obscured the intended meaning. The effect of the words of the dignified lama, as rendered into English by a scribe, entreating Almighty God to bless the celibate Father Victor's 'succeedings to third an' fourth generation' (116) is highly comic. In his turn, Father Victor sends letters to the lama, reporting on Kim's progress at school. The result is equally confusing, because, as the lama tells Kim: 'I do not well understand Sahib's letters. They must be interpreted to me' (208).

Before his formal education begins, Kim himself uses the services of a letter-writer. At the barrack school, although he can read a few words, he is mystified by white lines on a black board.

At St Xavier's he learns a 'magic worth anything else – he could write' (139). 'Writing' is indeed a 'magic' skill in a novel so much taken up with unravelling meaning. The secret service send their telegrams in code. Lurgan, besides teaching Kim the Koran and the right runes for administering drugs, 'wrote charms on parchment – elaborate pentagrams crowned with the names of devils' (185).

In its final stages, the plot of *Kim* revolves around a series of documents. There is Kim's note to Hurree Babu, carried inside a walnut shell by the Woman of Shamlegh. For her, the open shell is an erotic message, but Kim makes it an instrument, not of love, but of the Great Game. The note which he encloses is about more letters, those which the Russian was carrying. The hill-men, frightened by the written word, are thankful to hand them over to Kim. Once in his possession, they become an intolerable burden to him, until he is finally relieved of his load by Hurree Babu and can sleep in peace.

3.8 LEARNING AND KNOWING

The exploration of ways of learning is one of the hallmarks of Kipling's writing. Like Mowgli in *The Jungle Book* or Harvey Cheyne in *Captains Courageous*, the boy Kim is involved in a process of education. At the outset, Kim is almost illiterate. He has picked up a few writing lessons from a German painter, but has avoided formal schooling. Yet he knows a good deal. He 'knew the wonderful walled city of Lahore' and understood that the messages he carried involved 'intrigue': 'he knew that much, as he had known all evil since he could speak' (9). Some of Kim's knowledge has been acquired in order to survive, but he is also intensely curious. This is what first attracts his attention to the strange figure of the lama, from whom his companions shrink away in terror.

Knowledge is a key concept in the dialogue between the lama and the curator which follows. In the museum, a building devoted to the assimilation and dispersal of information, the curator, looking at the lama's face, changes his attitude in mid-sentence. 'I am here' he begins, but instead of saying 'to help', he concludes 'to gather knowledge' (13). And this is how it proves to be. He can show the lama photographs and sculptures, but, when the lama asks for information about the whereabouts of his river, the curator can only say: 'Alas, my brother, I do not know . . . If I knew, think you I would not cry it aloud?' (16–17).

This passage, more than any other, establishes the difference between the oriental and the European, not through sharp satire, but through an exploration of affinity:

> 'I do not know, I do not know.'
> The lama brought his thousand-wrinkled face once more a handsbreadth from the Englishman's. 'I see thou dost not know. Not being of the Law, the matter is hid from thee.'
> 'Ay, – hidden – hidden.'
> 'We are both bound, thou and I, my brother, But I' – he rose with a sweep of the soft thick drapery – 'I go to cut myself free. Come also!'
> 'I am bound', said the Curator (17).

The novel sets up a counterpoint between the lama's concept of knowledge, which is of the spirit, instinctual, and the book-learning of the European world, satirically parodied in Hurree Babu's account of his half-baked study of Shakespeare and Wordsworth. Kim's preference for mathematics is evidence of Kipling's admiration for the new, practical world, but Kipling, like Kim, is divided. In the final stages of the novel, other things are seen to be of much greater importance. The lama's river, the earth of India in which Kim lies and regains strength, these can communicate without the unsatisfactory and shifting intermediaries of learning and language.

3.9 PARENT AND CHILD

In certain respects Kim is a tribute from Rudyard Kipling to his own father, who appears in the novel, playing himself, the keeper of the 'Wonder House' (a translation of the vernacular word for museum). The lama's hope that Kim will 'be such a Sahib as he who gave me those spectacles' (136) is a curious linking of the inner and outer truth of *Kim*. Lockwood Kipling becomes not only the best that British India can offer, but also a model for the younger generation (Kim/Kipling) to emulate.

The part played by the keeper of the wonder house is comparatively brief. In the novel, he joins Kim's formidable collection of father-figures, among whom are the lama, Mahbub Ali and Colonel Creighton. According to Mahbub Ali, 'Half Hind' is disposed to see Kim as a son (307). Kim has been without his natural father for three years before the novel begins. Kimball O'Hara senior is recalled dimly by Kim, and more precisely by other characters like Father Victor. We learn that O'Hara left the army, worked on the railway, and died an opium addict. A failure in social terms, O'Hara was clearly more adequate as a parent. We hear of him with his baby son in his arms, and his provision of an amulet with documents eventually proves providential. The regiment, personified by Father Victor and Bennett, and the Masonic Lodge, in the person of Creighton, take up the responsibility for Kim's future.

The meaning of true fatherhood is love, and Kim's surrogate fathers are judged by their capacity to love him. All of them use the boy to some extent, reversing the normal pattern in which father provides for son. All of Kim's 'fathers' are compared with each other throughout the novel. His travels with the lama and with Mahbub Ali are contrasted with the journey which he takes with Creighton. Instead of warmth and reciprocal affection, this is marked by separation and division. Creighton sits in one carriage, Kim in another. The intellectual Creighton will bring the boy up, through education and forms of knowlege. The rumour of St Xavier's, that Creighton is Kim's father, is correct in this respect only.

Mahbub Ali also begins by using Kim as a tool, but comes to feel great warmth and affection for the boy. Like Creighton, he approves of the practical skills which Lurgan can teach, but, unlike Creighton, he sees no point in academic education. To him Kim is a colt to be trained, and he educates the boy in his own way, by experience and example. Mahbub can offer Kim what the lama cannot, the stimulation of excitement, and the essence of worldly enjoyment at its best. 'My son' (187) is Mahbub's address to Kim in Chapter 10, and later in the chapter, Kim responds with 'O my father' (193). In the end, Mahbub's love for Kim even enables him to overcome his jealousy of the lama: 'I call thee a good man – a very good man' (309) he concedes in the final chapter.

The novel traces the changing balance of protection between Kim and the lama. If at the opening, Kim takes on the paternal role, as the book progresses, the lama teaches him the things that really matter: selflessness, refusal of materialism, and – although the lama's faith would deny it – the power of human love.

It is important to realise that the lama also 'uses' Kim, whom he sees as vital to his own pursuit of salvation. In dream, the lama recognises that he cannot find his river without the boy. But, when he does find it, the suppressed father in the lama makes him turn back from nirvana to ensure the 'son's' salvation. The novel ends with sentences which, while capable of a religious interpretation, also put forward an earthly impulse – that of the father for the beloved child. This is the quality which the old soldier recognises in the lama: 'He is ashamed for that he has made a child happy. There was a very good householder lost in thee, my brother' (66).

Motherhood, and women in general, are pushed into last place in *Kim*. Kim's mother died early in his life, and he has no memory of her. The woman with whom he lives after his father's death is an opium addict who has let him run wild. Kim describes the lama as both 'father and mother and such all' (183), and it is only the old Ranee, herself a mother and grandmother, who finally draws the word 'Mother' from Kim, to her intense delight. In the previous chapter, Kim very nearly addresses the Woman of Shamlegh in this way, but recognises his mistake, and turns it to 'sister' instead. So young and attractive a woman cannot be a mother figure, although Kim, in his anxiety about her advances, may wish to categorise her in this way.

3.10 IDENTITY

In fiction, as in life, we identify characters by their names. In *Kim*, however, several characters have either no names, or, even more confusingly, several. We learn that the lama has a name only when he writes a letter, and he never asks Kim for his name, nor apparently uses it. The Ranee remains within the general group designated by her title, as the Rissaldar does within his. The Russian and the Frenchman are unidentified, like the vast mass of the Indian characters.

Namelessness is a professional device of the secret service. Even before he joins, Kim tells Creighton 'by the naming of names many good plans are brought to confusion' (129). When Kim first sees Hurree Babu, Lurgan asks him 'who he thought the man might be', and Kim replies 'God knows!' Lurgan accepts the answer, and goes on to tell Kim: 'it is noticeable that he has no name, but only a number and a letter – that is a custom among us' (175–6). This is not strictly true, although Hurree Babu's working name is indeed R17; Mahbub Ali is C25 and the agent on the train is E23.

Kim himself must learn that he is not simply 'Kim', and it is a mark of his absorption into the Sahib world that 'A priest clothed me and gave me a new name' (114). The faint biblical echoes are perhaps not entirely accidental. The divisions in Kim's personality have been discussed by several writers, and one has even described him as schizophrenic. The major split arises from his background. Orphaned at an early age, he is virtually homeless when the novel opens. While Kim remains in Lahore, or wanders with the lama, he is not conscious of divisions within himself, but when he is retrieved by the Mavericks and feels restrictions closing in around him, he begins to experience unhappiness. On the train from Umballa to Lucknow, alone in the compartment, Kim begins to see himself as an object:

> 'I go from one place to another as it might be a kick-ball. It is my *Kismet*. No man can escape his *Kismet*. But I am to pray to Bibi Miriam, and I am a Sahib.' He looked at his boots ruefully. 'No; I am Kim. This is the great world, and I am only Kim. Who is Kim?' He considered his own identity, a thing he had never done before, till his head swam. He was one insignificant person in all this roaring whirl of India, going southward to he knew not what fate (131).

In many ways, this is a common experience of adolescence, but, in its reference to the hugeness of India, Kim's identity crisis becomes a more universal experience. When the experience recurs it is once again on a railway journey. After leaving school, Kim is in the station at Lucknow, on his way to join the lama in Benares. Overwhelmed by a sense of loneliness, he asks, 'Who is Kim – Kim – Kim?' (202). The question is to some extent answered by his return to the lama.

Their second journey is a time of happiness. Lying in bed, Kim thinks of 'a great and a wonderful world – and I am Kim – Kim – Kim – alone – one person – in the middle of it all' (244). Intermittently, however, the demands of Kim's double life become oppressive. Carrying a gun while travelling with the pacifist lama, Kim is conscious of the thin ice over which he is passing. When he disguises and saves the Mahratta on the train, the lama warns him, with some reason, against the sin of pride. The narrator comments that Kim is able to keep silent, torn as he is between a wish to justify himself to the lama, and the secrecy enjoined by the great game. Having drawn the lama into spiritual and physical danger, Kim finds the incriminating letters a burden, like the Ancient Mariner's albatross round his neck. The breakdown which follows is not simply a result of physical exhaustion, but of continual mental tension and suppressed guilt.

Kim's recovery is marked by the repetition of the form of words in which he has questioned his identity. Walking out into the world, he looks at everything. ' "I am Kim. I am Kim. And what is Kim?" His soul repeated it again and again' (305). He throws himself onto the earth, and sleeps there. 'The ground was good clean dust – no new herbage that, living, is half-way to death already, but the hopeful dust that holds the seeds of all life' (306).

3.11 **THE SECRET GROUP**

Kipling's friendship with Beresford and Dunsterville at Westward Ho! established an ideal of the close-knit male group or secret society which continued to attract him. In adult life, he became a member of the Freemasons, a powerful male organisation sharing a common system of secret signs and passwords. Masonic ritual turns up in more than one of Kipling's stories, and here it is Kim's father's Masonic documents which establish his identity. Not all inner groups in Kipling's writing are Masonic, but a special language and unswerving loyalty are invariable elements in them. The three boys in *Stalky and Co.* develop their own systems of speech, and Mowgli, the outsider, has to learn the language of each group in the jungle. Without these passwords, he cannot survive.

The Sons of the Charm in *Kim* also have a system of passwords, and a secret sign, the turquoise amulet, by which they recognise each other. They are known by numbers, and maintain strict secrecy about their activities. Kim, already fascinated by intrigue, notices that Mahbub Ali and Creighton talk loudly about horses when they might be overheard, but change both their tone and their subject when alone. Creighton tests Kim's discretion by tempting him to declare that he knows the whereabouts of Creighton's house in Umballa. Kim, naturally discreet, passes this, and the other tests which Creighton sets with flying colours. Kipling's own style, with its tendency to encourage mystery through significant ellipses, is ideally suited to the interplay between these two. When Creighton suggests to Kim that he might be sent on survey work, and that others might warn him of dangers in the hill country, Kim replies that he would tell Creighton what was said.

> 'But if I answered: "I will give thee a hundred rupees for knowledge of what is behind those hills – for a picture of a river or a little news of what the people say in the villages there"?'
> 'How can I tell? I am only a boy. Wait till I am a man.' Then, seeing the Colonel's brow clouded, he went on: 'But I think I should in a few days earn the hundred rupees.'
> 'By what road?'
> Kim shook his head resolutely. 'If I said how I would earn them another man might hear and forestall me. It is not good to sell knowledge for nothing.'
> 'Tell now.' The Colonel held up a rupee. Kim's hand half reached towards it, and dropped.
> 'Nay, Sahib; nay. I know the price that will be paid for the answer, but I do not know why the question is asked' (131–2).

Throughout the early part of the novel, Kim seeks to disentangle the truth about the 'Great Game', waiting for Creighton, Mahbub Ali or Lurgan to speak directly. On the train to Lucknow, he drops a hint to Creighton about the message which he once carried to Umballa, and is told to remain silent. His two conversations with Mahbub Ali in Chapter 8 follow the same path, with each speaker dropping hints, and estimating the knowledge and motives of the other. In the end, it is the talkative Hurree Babu in

Chapters 10 and 12 who tells Kim what is happening, but, through the opacity of the Babu's language, the general air of mystery is maintained.

3.12 THE GREAT GAME

The designation of the Indian secret service as 'the Great Game' was not Kipling's invention. The phrase is thought to have been used first in connection with espionage on the northern frontiers in 1838. The expression, however, accurately reflects a part of Kipling's meaning in *Kim*. A 'game' is usually interpreted as a reference to children's play or to a sport. Kim himself plays cricket, and Mahbub Ali sells horses for polo. There are significant references in the novel to more informal children's games, like the struggle to sit on the gun, Zam-Zammah, the Lahore equivalent of 'king-of-the-castle', or the singing game with rosary beads which the lama plays to amuse the small child in Chapter 3.

In these two passages, both involving young children, Kipling cleverly introduces 'games' to comment on what is essentially serious, the divisions in India, and the affectionate nature of the lama. The other 'games' of Kim are more consciously instructive, and less revealing. Kim's education with Lurgan takes the form of a series of games, but the fun is subsumed into the competitive element. When Kim and the Hindu boy 'play' at remembering the stones on the tray, or at dressing up, they are actually experiencing an intensive course of training.

In most games one of two things is happening. Either, as in cricket and polo, there are predetermined rules, or, as when Kim is sitting on the gun, one player takes control of the proceedings, setting himself in judgement over the other or others. The wider interpretation of a game, as a way of life, has been analysed by Eric Berne in *Games People Play*: 'Pastimes and games are the substitutes for the real living of real intimacy.'

From early in the currency of the phrase, 'the Great Game' was associated with chess. Kipling's game-imagery in *Kim* does not suggest chess so much as poker. 'Would it be safe to return the Colonel's lead?' (131), wonders Kim, or responding with pleasure to Creighton's secrecy: 'Here was a man after his own heart – a tortuous and indirect person playing a hidden game' (130). In his

Lahore days, Kim loved 'the game for its own sake' (9), and is 'Irish enough . . . to reckon silver the least part of any game' (45).

The reader is left to ponder whether there is not something immature in the playing of the Great Game, a retreat from reality of the kind which Berne describes. Certainly the stakes are high, E23 is genuinely in danger of losing his life, and the invasion of India by the Russians seems to be a real political threat. Kipling, however, makes comparatively little of these things. It is fun to outwit your enemies by guile, as Kim, the descendant of the earlier Stalky, soon discovers. The game, however, ceases to be a game and becomes deadly earnest when the Russian hits the lama. The moment when the Great Game impinges physically upon the emotional meaning of the novel is also the one when the game becomes a sickening burden, represented by the letters which nearly overwhelm Kim altogether. Discussion of the issue reveals a division in Kipling as a writer. Personally, he admired strong stern emotionless Englishmen like Creighton and Strickland, the masters of the Great Game, but, intuitively, he grasped their limitations. The treatment of the 'game' in *Kim* is yet another indication of profound divisions in its author's thinking.

4 TECHNICAL FEATURES

4.1 PICARESQUE

In structure and content, *Kim* belongs to more than one genre of novel. As a novel dealing with a journey or quest, it can be described as 'picaresque'. The term derives from the Spanish, 'picaro', a rogue, and the master-work of the form is *Don Quixote* (1605 and 1615) by Miguel de Cervantes (1547–1616). Kipling himself acknowledged the debt to Cervantes in *Something of Myself*: 'As to its [*Kim*'s] form there was but one possible to the author, who said that what was good enough for Cervantes was good enough for him'. Don Quixote's quest for knightly accomplishment is undertaken, like the lama's search for his river, with a total concentration of body and mind. The lama is not, like Don Quixote, an object of satire, but both are vulnerable men, guided through a dangerous world by a knowing younger companion.

Kipling must have known the significant English contributions to the picaresque genre. One related work is John Bunyan's *Pilgrim's Progress* (1678), describing a group of characters travelling towards salvation, their final obstacle being the river of death. More strictly picaresque is *Joseph Andrews* (1742) by Henry Fielding (1707–54), where the young hero accompanies an unworldly clergyman, Abraham Adams, on a journey from London to the country, running the gauntlet of dishonest innkeepers and irreligious clergymen. The protagonist of *Pickwick Papers* (1837) by Charles Dickens (1812–70) is another benevolent but incompetent older man, Mr Pickwick, whose cockney servant, Sam Weller, is, like Cervantes's Sancho Panza and Fielding's Joseph Andrews, a precursor of Kim.

Picaresque fiction characteristically introduces and discards characters encountered along the way. These vividly drawn and frequently humorous people appear briefly, not making a sufficiently extended appearance to demand complexity of characterisation. Dickens's significant contribution to the picaresque, as he developed it through his early novels, was to reintroduce such figures, and so bring the work to a rounded conclusion in which most play some part. *Kim* follows Dickens to a considerable extent. Kim and the lama meet the old soldier and the Ranee at the beginning of the novel, and return to them later. The characters of the espionage plot, Mahbub Ali, Hurree Babu and Creighton, all reappear at intervals. The part played by some minor characters; the Jat with his son, or the Hindu holy man, however, is confined to a single episode. Two others, who seem to fall into this category, in fact have a continued existence in other works by Kipling; Strickland, the policeman on the Grand Trunk Road, and Lispeth, the Woman of Shamlegh, amongst them.

4.2 BILDUNGSROMAN

Kim is also a novel of a young person's development, in the manner of the German *bildungsroman* (building novel) initiated by Goethe (1749–1832) in *Wilhelm Meister* (1786 onwards). The form was popular in nineteenth-century England, and often introduced an element of autobiography. *Pendennis* (1850) by W. M. Thackeray (1811–63) and *David Copperfield* (1850) by Charles Dickens are well-known examples.The worldly Kim is not as innocent or as vulnerable as these heroes, but he has to learn to understand himself and to find the maturity to make the choices which lie before him.

Kim's education is one measure of his growth, but a truer one is the boy's developing ability to transcend self through his love for the lama. When Father Victor questions Kim about his own future: 'Kim saw nothing save a vision of the lama going south in a train with none to beg for him' (117). In the crisis of the lama's distress after the Russian's attack, Kim offers himself in propitiation: 'Holy One, thou are innocent of all evil. May I be thy sacrifice!' (282). As a declaration of love this almost equals the lama's sacrifice of nirvana at the end of the novel.

The *bildungsroman* hero often establishes his claim to maturity by marrying the right girl in the end, having recognised the errors of earlier loves and illusions. At the end of *Kim*, the hero is only 16 and still at the outset of life. Although his attractive appearance and his future appeal for women are mentioned more than once, Kim himself recalls women's approaches with embarrassment. In rejecting the advances of the Woman of Shamlegh, however, he notes a significant change: 'At least she did not treat me like a child' (288).

The narrator comments on the precocity of those brought up in the heat of India. In Mahbub Ali's eyes Kim is a man long before his companions have left St Xavier's, and even the St Xavier's boys are far more mature than their contemporaries in England. The price to be paid, however, is the 'half-collapse that sets in at twenty-two or twenty-three' (138).

The hero's usual choice between two women, the wrong and the right, is replaced here by a choice between two ways of living, the Great Game and the lama's Middle Way. At the end of the novel, the hero has gained in wisdom, but he never makes a final choice between the opposed worlds, and it is left to us to decide whether either is right. Kipling's father asked him: 'Did *it* stop, or you?' and told 'that it was *It*'. 'Then it oughtn't to be too bad' was Lockwood Kipling's reply. Critics of the book have either assumed that they understood Kipling's real meaning, or have complained that he should have made it clearer. The classic *bildungsroman* ends with the hero looking forward to a settled and constructive future. The ending of *Kim* is more 'open' and 'modern' in its refusal to close off ambiguities.

4.3 **THE ADVENTURE STORY**

Kim belongs to a third genre of fiction – the adventure story. Some of the classics of this form were published in the late Victorian and Edwardian period, building upon a tradition begun by Captain Marryat (1792–1848) and R. M. Ballantyne (1825–94). Among them are *Treasure Island* (1883) and *Kidnapped* (1886) by Robert Louis Stevenson (1850–94); *King Solomon's Mines* (1886) and *She* (1887) by Kipling's friend, Henry Rider Haggard (1856–1925); and *The Four Feathers* (1902) by A. E. W. Mason (1865–1948). G. A. Henty (1832–1902) was a prolific author of books for boys, many dealing with the military campaigns of the past.

Most of these adventures take place outside Britain, exploiting a taste for the foreign and exotic which has been a feature of English literature since the Middle Ages. The translation of *The Arabian Nights* into French at the end of the eighteenth century stimulated a new wave of orientalism, and Kim's place in this tradition is acknowledged in the first chapter, which tells us that Kim's life was 'wild as that of the Arabian Nights'. He was 'hand in glove with men who led lives stranger than anything Haroun al Raschid [the Caliph of *The Arabian Nights*] dreamed of' (9).

There are a number of episodes in *Kim* which can be readily related to the adventure tradition. When Kim, working against time, succeeds in disguising the Mahratta and so rescuing him from his enemies, or when he carries a message to Umballa which results in army mobilisation, we can recognise the familiar situation in which a boy triumphs over experienced adult foes. The defeat and humiliation of the Russian spies satisfies the same wish to see the over-confident enemy confounded by the determination and will-power of the hero and his companions. That this is an inadequate reading of *Kim* is obvious, but these patterns are an important element in the plot.

In its treatment of espionage and counter-espionage, *Kim* moves beyond the simple adventure story into the newer subspecies of the spy story. Sinister figures involved with hostile continental powers or revolutionary organisations appear in the fiction of Dickens and Wilkie Collins (1824–89), but *Kim* is one of the first true spy stories.

In the later spy fiction of Ian Fleming and John Le Carré, we are made aware of a code which is, to some extent, shared by both sides in the game of espionage. In seeking to outwit each other, the rival groups are not so much preoccupied with ideologies, as with the exercise of their own skill. Kipling, writing in an earlier age, endows only the British with this quality. Of his two foreign spies, the Frenchman is recognisably a gentleman and a restraining influence, but the real threat, the Russian, is beyond the pale. He scorns the religious scruples of others, hits the lama, and so earns the public scorn to which Hurree Babu exposes him. This is counter-espionage made easy; when the other side are wholly despicable.

4.4 REALISM

As a young author, Kipling was praised for his realistic accounts of India, a country with which many in Britain were associated, but to which few would ever actually go. Comparison between one of the squalid accounts of Lahore given in Kipling's journalism, written for an Anglo-Indian audience, and a passage from Chapter 1 of *Kim* will indicate the extent to which Kipling is doing something different here, stressing the excitement and drama of India, rather than its dirt and disease:

> Voices of children singing their lessons at school; sounds of feet on stone steps, or wooden balconies over-head; voices raised in argument, or conversation, sounded dead and muffled as though they came through wool; and it seemed as if, at any moment, the tide of unclean humanity might burst through its dam of rotten brickwork and filth-smeared wood, blockading the passages below. Nor was this impression removed when we turned out of the gully into a third courtyard surrounded by a mass of ruinous houses, thus taking the pent up army on the flank, as it were . . . By unclean corners of walls; on each step of ruinous staircases; on the roofs of low out-houses; by window, and housetop, or stretched amid garbage unutterable, this section of Lahore was awaking to another day's life ('Typhoid at Home', 1885).

> what he loved was the game for its own sake – the stealthy prowl through the dark gullies and lanes, the crawl up a water-pipe, the sights and sounds of the women's world on the flat roofs, and the headlong flight from housetop to housetop under cover of the hot dark. Then there were holy men, ash-smeared *fakirs* by their brick shrines under the trees at the riverside, with whom he was quite familiar – greeting them as they returned from begging-tours, and, when no one was by, eating from the same dish (9).

This is perhaps to overstate the case. The first passage was written in 1885, the second ten or more years later, when Kipling was no longer living in India. Journalism and fiction make very different demands. It is clear, however, that Kipling, for all his mass of detail, and his consultations with his father, produces a general and not a specific picture of life in northern India in *Kim*. The heat, of which Kipling often complains in journalism and private letters, is not a problem for Kim, until he dresses in European clothes. The hill-town of Simla, of which Kipling had often written, is again treated impressionistically in Chapter 8:

> He led the horses below the main road into the lower Simla bazar – the crowded rabbit-warren that climbs up from the valley to the Town Hall at an angle of forty-five. A man who knows his way there can defy all the police of India's summer capital, so cunningly does veranda communicate with veranda, alley-way with alley-way, and bolt-hole with bolt-hole. Here live those who minister to the wants of the glad city – *jhampanis* who pull the pretty ladies' rickshaws by night and gamble till the dawn; grocers, oil-sellers, curio-vendors, firewood-dealers, priests, pickpockets, and native employees of the Government. Here are discussed by courtesans the things which are supposed to be profoundest secrets of the India Council; and here gather all the sub-sub-agents of half the Native States (161–2).

Here Kipling chooses to stress the crowded and secretive aspects of the town. He hints at sexual adventure ('pretty ladies', 'courtesans'); he refers to gambling and espionage, and, behind it all, to the political power of the India Council. Contemporary photographs of Simla both confirm and deny the impression of the passage. The cramped houses on the steep hillsides are immediately apparent, but there is a general air of relaxation and holiday-making, closer to Kipling's own early Simla stories than to the slightly sinister picture he paints in *Kim*.

4.5 CHARACTERISATION

The most telling thing about the characters in *Kim* is their multiplicity. In an attempt to convey the sense of teeming life in

India, Kipling includes a mass of different figures, representative of many races, religions, castes and ways of life. The main characters stand out from this sense of teeming life; the lama, Mahbub Ali, Creighton, the old soldier, the Ranee, and, above all, Kim himself.

As the hero of the novel, **Kim** is also the most omnipresent character, and the most interesting. Kipling's presentation of a young boy, making his own way in the huge subcontinent of India, is a triumphant achievement, and by no means an easy one. Kipling greatly admired Robert Browning (1812–89), whose long dramatic poem, *Pippa Passes* (1841) provides a revealing comparison with *Kim*. Pippa is the young girl who passes through the city, singing 'God's in his heaven – all's right with the world!'. As the poem shows, all is far from right with the world. Kim, like Pippa, is a 'Little Friend of all the World', but his ability to keep alive by intrigue and scrounging prevents any accumulation of sentiment around the epithet. Too much sweetness is also kept at bay by Kim's rebelliousness. He sits on the forbidden gun, and, if annoyed, throws out appalling verbal pedigrees at transgressors.

As a character, Kim develops through the novel. There is a clearly discernible difference between the confident Kim who sets out with the lama in Chapter 1, simply because the idea of travel interests him, and the self-questioning, thoughtful youth who undertakes the second, and successful, quest for the lama's river. As with other characters, Kipling makes considerable use of dialogue to define Kim's character. It is noticeable, for example, that Kim abandons pidgin English after going to St Xavier's, and that his conversations with the lama are conducted in a far more open and direct spirit than those with Creighton or even with Mahbub Ali.

Many of the episodes are seen, not through straightforward narration, but through the eyes and the consciousness of Kim himself. In certain passages, this involves a deliberate limitation of viewpoint, producing a framed, pictorial effect, which suggests the limitations of the boy's understanding. When the lama talks with the museum curator, Kim eavesdrops through a hole in the door, but finds 'most of the talk was altogether above his head' (14) and goes to sleep. Kipling adopts the same device when Kim looks through 'a knot-hole in the planking' (32) while the man from Delhi searches Mahbub Ali's property. At Umballa, he crawls close to Creighton's house to look through the windows, and, soon afterwards, lies on his stomach to watch the regiment at dinner in the mess-tent. Here Kipling makes ironic play with Kim's misconceptions about the regimental symbol, a golden bull standing at the centre of the table. 'It was as he suspected. The Sahibs prayed to their God' (95). In the context of British disdain for Hindu cow-worship, the joke is a good one.

Creating the **lama** was an achievement to match Kipling's success with Kim. It is notoriously difficult to persuade a reader to like, or even to believe in, a good character. Dickens sometimes succeeds with eccentric or half-witted characters, as does the Russian writer, Feodor Dostoevsky (1821–81). Myshkin, the hero of Dostoevsky's *The Idiot* of 1866 has been described as a 'holy fool', and, in the early chapters of *Kim*, the lama has some affinities with him. Both preserve their saintly innocence in a world of violence and corruption, but only through an apparent incapacity to understand what is going on in a worldly sense. In both cases, this innocence is associated with religious imagery and belief.

As the novel proceeds, however, it begins to be clear that the lama is not as impractical as he seems. During the conversation with Father Victor and Bennett, he is not only able to distinguish between the 'good man' and the 'fool', but sees at once the importance of sending Kim to the best school available. Writing to Father Victor, through a scribe, to arrange for Kim to go to St Xavier's, the lama utters two memorable sentences: '*Education is greatest blessing if of best sorts. Otherwise no earthly use*' (116). This could stand as a motto for the novel. He then arranges for his monastery to pay Kim's school bills, leaving Creighton to wonder how he has managed to do it.

A conflict between action and passivity, often a feature of Kipling's work, is present, not only in the plot of *Kim*, but within the lama himself. Trained to accept experience passively, the lama intermittently finds himself faced with a temptation to assert a hold upon life. When he loses Kim to the Mavericks, the lama's lament is deeply moving, a cry of love for Kim, and an expression of deep despair for his own failings:

'I delighted in the sight of life, the new people upon the roads, and in thy joy at seeing these things. I was pleased with thee who should have considered my Search and my Search alone. Now I am sorrowful because thou art taken away and my River is far from me. It is the Law which I have broken' (104).

At the time of the meeting with the Russian and the Frenchman, the lama is again inwardly divided. When the Russian hits him, the old man is suddenly overwhelmed by anger, and, during the night which follows, he endures agonies of remorse, not only for his aggressive impulses, but also for coming into the hills which he loves, and for leaving the plains where his quest should have taken him. Joining the men of Shamlegh, the lama makes his farewell to the hills, 'as a dying man blesses his folk' (280). Then, speaking to Kim alone, the old man confesses his fault, and accepts the message of the blow: ' "Back to the path", says the Blow. "The Hills are not for thee. Thou canst not choose freedom and go in bondage to the delight of life" ' (283).

If the lama gives *Kim* its greatness and its depth, **Mahbub Ali** gives the novel much of its oriental colour. Kipling surrounds him with the evocative power of names, and associates him with the 'mysterious land beyond the Passes of the North' (25). His belt is from Bokhariot, his horses from Balkh, Kabul and Kathiawar. Mahbub Ali likes rich food, fine clothes and women. He boasts to Kim of having killed a man and fathered a man before he was 16.

Like the lama, Mahbub Ali is old, but he is still caught up in the romance of the dangerous. His life is threatened twice in the novel, when he is searched in Lahore, and when two men lie in wait for him beside the railway line in Umballa. On both occasions, he is saved by Kim, to whom he becomes deeply attached. The lama and Mahbub Ali are as different as Kipling can make them, the ascetic and the *bon viveur*, the man of meditation and the man of the world. Yet the two men, taken together, represent life itself, the extremes which stand for choice, but also for the wholeness of man's experience.

Like other characters in *Kim*, Mahbub Ali was drawn from life. On 19 January 1886, Kipling contributed his regular column, 'A Week in Lahore', to *The Civil and Military Gazette*. The subject on this occasion was the Sultan Serai in Lahore, and an Afghan horse-dealer called Afzul. Afzul possessed much of the extrovert, larger-than-life quality of Mahbub Ali, but was apparently no more than a shrewd salesman. Kipling, however, resisted his incitement to buy an Arab grey.

It has been suggested that the original of **Colonel Creighton** was Captain, later Lieutenant Colonel, Alexander Herbert Mason, whom Kipling would have known in Lahore. Like Creighton, Mason was a surveyor attached to the Intelligence department in the north. In the novel, Creighton is a mysterious figure, but a commanding one. His understanding of the country immediately gives him an opening into what, to the less-well-informed, seems an arcane area of knowledge. His subordinates treat him with considerable respect, and even Kim finds it necessary to approach him with caution. Creighton's intellectual curiosity is his dominant quality. He is not merely concealing his true feeling when he says that he finds Kim an interesting specimen. Only once do we hear an inner truth of Creighton: 'deep in his heart . . . lay the ambition to write "F.R.S." [Fellow of the Royal Society] after his name' (191).

When he discovers that **Hurree Chunder Mookerjee** has the same ambition, Creighton thinks better of him. Hurree Babu is a Bengali, one of a race for whom Kipling generally had little enthusiasm. In his annotations for *Kim*, Brigadier Mason suggests that Hurree Babu was partly drawn from Sarat Chandra Das, 'one of the Pundits of the Survey Department, who was a keen ethnologist'. Kipling's ambivalent attitude to the education of Indians emerges in the parody acount of Hurree Babu's education. He recommends to Kim a few Shakespeare plays, Wordsworth's *The Excursion*, and 'the eminent authors Burke and Hare' (179). Burke and Hare were notorious murderers, and Hurree Babu has muddled them with the Irish writer Edmund Burke (1729–97) and the travel writer and autobiographer Augustus Hare (1834–1903). In his conversations with Kim, Hurree Babu's English is pretentious and almost meaningless, while, when he shifts to the vernacular, he speaks with clarity and authority.

In playing a part with the foreign spies, Hurree Babu complains of his position under a government which 'forced upon him a white man's education and neglected to supply him with a white man's salary' (257–8). The point is a good one, but there is no reason to suppose that Kipling is making it. Indeed, when he notes that the spies gave Hurree Babu a drink and invited him to eat with them, this is a point against, not for, them. 'The Englishman is not, as a

rule, familiar with the Asiatic' (257), even though, unlike the spies, he does not hit a friendly Indian under little provocation.
Lurgan is a character with a well-documented original, a seller of curiosities in Simla called Alexander M. Jacob. Jacob was a Turkish or Persian Moslem, who particularly dealt in precious stones. Jacob, who was well known to visitors to Simla, was the subject of another novel, *Mr Isaacs* by F. Marion Crawford (1882). In *Kim*, Lurgan with his gift for hypnosis and his strange household, is at the heart of all the intrigue of Simla. A man of remarkable and rather alarming human insight, he adds a striking element to the adventure plot.

Kim reflects the dominance of the male in Kipling's India. Only two women play a large part in the novel, the Ranee and the Woman of Shamlegh, and neither is of major importance in the plot. Surprisingly, both are women of power and position, the Ranee as a rich widow, the Woman of Shamlegh as the ruler of a hill community where women stand above men in the hierarchy. Both characters, however, have a 'female' role in the novel. For very different reasons, they feed and protect Kim and the lama, and they respond to his physical attraction, whether as would-be mother or lover.

The **Ranee** is in awe of the lama, but also exploits him, talking incessantly, and demanding charms for members of her family. This is a recognisable character type, the tiresome and strong-willed old woman, who turns out to have a heart of gold. There is much humour in the lama's nervous fear of her.

Lispeth, **the Woman of Shamlegh**, is younger and more cynical. Readers of Kipling's early short story, 'Lispeth' (1888) will know that she was brought up by a clergyman and his wife, and fell in love with an Englishman, whom she expected to marry. In her disappointment, she abandoned European ways, and returned to her own people. Lispeth refers to her past in a conversation with Kim, whom she associates with her lost sahib: 'I thought it was my Sahib come back, and he was my God' (286).

Lispeth is the hard and unyielding local ruler in a community which practises polyandry (plurality of husbands). She has little time for religion, and treats her husbands with scorn, ordering them to travel many miles as bearers of the lama. Kim's attitude to her beauty is described in a curious and negative phrase which suggests his confusion of mind: ' "I am a priest." ' Kim had recovered himself, and, the woman being aught but unlovely, thought best to stand on his office' (276). The reader's sympathy is likely to be with the woman in the scene where she first sets out to attract Kim, and then turns from him in disappointment, speaking with distaste of her life among the hill-men and women. Her parting with Kim is a fleeting moment of romance, as he, responding to her feeling, salutes her, as a sahib, with a kiss.

4.6 NARRATION

Kipling does not personalise, nor draw attention to his narrator, but certain assumptions can be made about him. We may deduce from his occasional references to files and documents that he is connected with the secret service. Kim's report and scale plan of Bikanir, made with the help of a rosary, 'was on hand a few years ago (a careless clerk filed it with the rough notes of E23's second Seistan survey), but by now the pencil characters must be almost illegible' (186–7). When the narrator tells us that he has studied Kim's school report, or assumes a familiar knowledge of what goes on in a character's mind – 'Kim will remember till he dies that long, lazy journey from Umballa' (160) – these devices appear as part of a strategy to suggest the factual truth of Kim's story, to imply that this is a biographical not a fictional undertaking. The reader, on his part, is assumed to be easily bored, at least about Kim's schooldays: 'Therefore you would scarcely be interested in Kim's experiences as a St Xavier's boy' (136) or 'The record of a boy's education interests few save his parents, and, as you know, Kim was an orphan' (180).

These last examples are a device by which Kipling can avoid writing on subjects which he does not intend to include, but the other passages quoted above raise unanswered questions. Is the narrator telling the story because Kim is now a famous or heroic figure in the secret service? Or is their inclusion here only another aspect of the book's preoccupation with the mysterious qualities of the written word?

4.7 KIPLING'S PROSE

The prose style of *Kim* is remarkably economical, and often highly compressed. In contrast to his contemporaries, Henry James and

Marcel Proust, Kipling had no time for the long sentence, or for extended subordinate clauses. His hallmarks are strong verbs and direct statement. Yet Kipling's prose is by no means simple or straightforward. He is as far from the pellucid clarity of George Orwell as he is from the complexity of James. His characteristic compression can make Kipling's prose difficult to read, and, if *Kim* is more readily understood than some of his other works, it is by no means a novel without difficulties.

One indication of the amount which is compressed into a comparatively short book is the existence of Brigadier A. Mason's notes on *Kim*, published by the Kipling Society. Mason's work, which covers 150 pages, explains most of the Indian references in *Kim*, and is in itself a startling revelation of the density of the novel. On a smaller scale, most editions of *Kim* include a useful glossary of several hundred terms, most of them linguistic, historical or geographical, all of which might be presumed to be unfamiliar to the British reader. While this material is unlikely to cause serious delays, its presence makes a noticeable difference to the experience of reading. About half of the novel's pages have at least one word in italics, the means by which Kipling usually signifies an Indian term.

Nor is Kipling's English entirely straightforward. His phraseology is often noticeably archaic, reminiscent of the language of the Authorised Version of the Bible (1611). When the cultivator's wife complains that the lama ignores her and asks whether Kim will do the same:

> 'Nay, mother,' said Kim most promptly. 'Not when the woman is well-looking and above all charitable to the hungry.'
> 'A beggar's answer,' said the Sikh laughing. 'Thou has brought it on thyself, sister!' Kim's hands were crooked in supplication.
> 'And whither goest thou?' said the woman, handing him the half of a cake from a greasy package.
> 'Even to Benares.'
> 'Jugglers belike?' the young soldier suggested. 'Have ye any tricks to pass the time? Why does not that yellow man answer?'
> 'Because', said Kim stoutly, 'he is holy, and thinks upon matters hidden from thee.' (36–7).

Here, in a few lines, Kipling uses a number of expressions

which, when he wrote, were either archaic or would have occurred only in English rural dialects. Unlike other European languages, modern English has no intimate form of the second person singular. Kipling's use of 'thee', 'thou' and 'ye', whenever characters are speaking in the Indian vernacular, both supplies this missing element, and also sets off 'Indian' speech from formal English. 'Belike', 'whither goest', 'even' (meaning directly), and 'well-looking', are all forms of words no longer in common usage. Taken with Kipling's compressed and Latinate use of the phrase 'matters hidden from thee', where another writer would have said 'matters which are hidden from thee', the details of the passage convey an indirect recollection of seventeenth-century English prose.

At times there are more direct references to the Bible. When Kim tries to get the better of the Ranee, 'this was a bow drawn at a venture' (78, and *I Kings*, xxii, 34); Mahbub gives Kim 'the same sort of advice as his mother gave to Lemuel' (193), in other words, he tells him to avoid drunkenness and the entanglements of women (*Proverbs*, xxxi).

Another favourite Kipling device is the compound word. *Kim* is scattered with these, an indication of the writer's struggle to find the right word. Where Henry James fought against the imprecision of language by endlessly qualifying his terms, Kipling, characteristically, worked at it until he found a reasonably satisfactory solution. His compounds are created by combining two words with a hyphen between them. Placed in visual juxtaposition in this way, the coinage has a subtly different meaning from that of the separated parts.

In the penultimate paragraph of Chapter 1, for example, Kim speaks of 'that made-up horse-lie' (33), thus turning his mission for Mahbub Ali into a single concept, with three of its four elements signifying duplicity. Later in the same paragraph, Kim wakes the 'light-sleeping' lama, a different thing from the lama 'who was sleeping lightly'. The use of a double-compound, resulting in an even more compact and forceful construction, is common in Kim. The Ranee is first introduced as a 'strong-tongued, iron-willed old lady' (75), and the account of the Grand Trunk Road makes extensive use of the same device. Arriving there, Kim and the lama 'looked at the green-arched, shade-flecked length of it, the white breadth speckled with slow-pacing folk; and the two-roomed police-station opposite' (67). Most remarkable of all is the sentence which describes a group of women railway workers: 'a flat-footed, big-bosomed, strong-limbed, blue-petticoated clan of earth-carriers, hurrying north on news of a job, and wasting no time by the road' (72).

The Grand Trunk Road passage illustrates another, related, aspect of Kipling's prose, his use of language and description which give the impression of being more than usually dense upon the page. Hosts of details follow close on each other like the brilliantly illuminated passages of a pre-Raphaelite painting. As group follows group along the road, the narrator touches off the descriptions with a brief account of dress, jewellery or accoutrements. As the bride passes, there is a sound of 'music and shoutings, and a smell of marigold and jasmine stronger even than the reek of the dust' (72). Yet the vividness of separate areas does not detract from the sense of the whole, as the controlled and insistent power of the prose rhythm carries the reader steadily through the passage, finally returning to where it began, in the relationship between Kim and the lama:

> From time to time the lama took snuff, and at last Kim could endure the silence no longer.
> 'This is a good land – the land of the South!' said he. 'The air is good; the water is good. Eh?'
> 'And they are all bound upon the Wheel,' said the lama. 'Bound from life after life. To none of those has the Way been shown' (73–4).

The capitalisation of 'Wheel' and 'Way' in this passage is another strategy by which Kipling focuses attention on certain key issues. These words, together with 'Road' and, in the second, though not the first, part of the novel, 'Great Game', are often set apart as terms signifying a special, even mystic, quality. Other religious expressions and epithets (Friend of all the World, Holy One) are regularly written with capital letters, but do not have the same special force. Each of these four terms stands for a way of reading life: the Buddhist Wheel, the Way of the disciple, the Road, with its implications of endless travel and of freedom from restriction, the Great Game, with its group loyalties and rules. By accumulating deposits of meaning these capitalised words become another kind of economy. The author only has to repeat them to set off a chain of associations and reactions.

With few exceptions, the imagery of *Kim* is drawn from fields appropriate to the novel's subject. Most of the many similes refer to rural and animal life, with the characters turning naturally to those animals which they know best: for the Jat farmer, Jats, when crossed, can be bad-tempered 'like our own buffaloes' (214); to the Woman of Shamlegh, the Babu is 'like a strayed buffalo in a cornfield . . . snorting and sneezing with cold' (284); the lama, in his despair, compares himself to 'a strayed yak' (283). Mahbub Ali sees everything in relation to the behaviour of horses, most memorably when he describes Kim to Creighton as though he were a polo pony. Elsewhere, he compares Kim's fate to a carpet, a craft associated with his native Afghanistan, 'Children should not see a carpet on the loom until the pattern is made plain' (123).

The narrator also invokes animal parallels. 'The lama dropped wearily to the ground, much as a heavy fruit-eating bat cowers' (76); hookahs, 'in full blast sound like bull-frogs' (82); the women workers on the Grand Trunk Road are a 'solid line of blue, rising and falling like the back of a caterpillar in haste' (72): Kim is 'as methodical as an old hunter in matters of the road' (276). Occasionally, the similes are drawn from a far wider field. When Kim drops the surveying instruments from the window: 'The theodolite hit a jutting cliff-ledge and exploded like a shell; the books, inkstands, paint-boxes, compasses, and rulers showed for a few seconds like a swarm of bees' (275–6). The hungry Kim looks like 'the young saint of a stained-glass window' (213), and, in another ecclesiastical image, the narrator tells us that the lama is no more likely to part 'with his chart to a casual wayfarer than an archbishop would pawn the holy vessels of his cathedral' (262).

4.8 AUDIENCE

Kim has sometimes been regarded as a book for boys, an attitude reinforced by the film adaptations. In my discussion, I have assumed that *Kim* is a novel, not a children's book. The complexity of the issues raised in this guide must, to some degree, confirm this judgement. Even Kipling's acknowledged books for children, *The Jungle Book* and *The Just So Stories*, work on two interlocked levels, one of which is apparent to the child reader, while the other is presented to the more knowing adult. *Kim* is too difficult for a young child, but accessible to an adolescent, who will readily identify with a character of his own age.

In consulting one 14-year-old boy about his reactions to *Kim*, I was surprised by his unprompted awareness of some of the critical issues most often raised. For this reader, *Kim* was a book with two meanings, the adventure plot, and the deeper level beneath. Reacting to Kipling's habit of ellipsis (making oblique rather than complete reference) he experienced initial difficulties in understanding what lay behind certain things, giving the significance of the five northern kings and the status of the Ranee as examples. He enjoyed reading the book, which he found colourful and picturesque, but felt that the plot was badly constructed, 'jumped about' and ended in too much of a hurry. Kim, he decided, was too idealistic to become a spy.

As a schoolboy himself, he was disappointed that Kipling skipped over Kim's schooldays, and was pleased when Lurgan taught Kim not to be 'too cocky'. Having touched on Buddhism in a school course on world religions, he found Kipling's version 'wishy-washy'. In a series of reactions unlikely among readers in 1901, he complained that Kipling had not placed enough emphasis upon women, felt that the anti-Russian stance was excessive and that the Russian was a caricature. More surprisingly, he speculated on whether the British in India were as bad as Kipling had painted them.

5 SPECIMEN PASSAGE AND COMMENTARY

5.1 SPECIMEN PASSAGE

Behind them an angry farmer brandished a bamboo pole. He was a market-gardener, Arain by caste, growing vegetables and flowers for Umballa city, and well Kim knew the breed.

'Such an one,' said the lama, disregarding the dogs, 'is impolite to strangers, intemperate of speech and uncharitable. Be warned by his demeanour, my disciple.'

'Ho, shameless beggars!' shouted the farmer. 'Begone! Get hence!'

'We go,' the lama returned, with quiet dignity. 'We go from these unblessed fields.'

'Ah,' said Kim, sucking in his breath. 'If the next crop fail, thou canst only blame thine own tongue.'

The man shuffled uneasily in his slippers. 'The land is full of beggars,' he began, half apologetically.

'And by what sign didst thou know that we would beg from thee, O Mali?' said Kim tartly, using the name that a market-gardener least likes. 'All we sought was to look at that river beyond the field there.'

'River, forsooth!' the man snorted. 'What city do ye hail from not to know a canal-cut? It runs as straight as an arrow, and I pay for the water as though it were molten silver. There is a branch of a river beyond. But if ye need water I can give that – and milk.'

'Nay, we will go to the river,' said the lama, striding out.

'Milk and a meal,' the man stammered, as he looked at the

strange tall figure. 'I – I would not draw evil upon myself – or my crops. But beggars are so many in these hard days.'

'Take notice.' The lama turned to Kim. 'He was led to speak harshly by the Red Mist of anger. That clearing from his eyes, he becomes courteous and of an affable heart. May his fields be blessed! Beware not to judge men too hastily, O farmer.'

'I have met holy ones who would have cursed thee from hearthstone to byre,' said Kim to the abashed man. 'Is he not wise and holy? I am his disciple.'

He cocked his nose in the air loftily and stepped across the narrow field-borders with great dignity.

'There is no pride,' said the lama, after a pause, 'there is no pride among such as follow the Middle Way.'

'But thou hast said he was low-caste and discourteous.'

'Low-caste I did not say, for how can that be which is not? Afterwards he amended the discourtesy, and I forgot the offence. Moreover, he is as we are, bound upon the Wheel of Things; but he does not tread the way of deliverance.' He halted at a little runlet among the fields, and considered the hoof-pitted bank.

'Now, how wilt thou know thy River?' said Kim, squatting in the shade of some tall sugar-cane.

'When I find it, an enlightenment will surely be given. This, I feel, is not the place. O littlest among the waters, if only thou couldst tell me where runs my River! But be thou blessed to make the fields bear!'

'Look! Look!' Kim sprang to his side and dragged him back. A yellow-and-brown streak glided from the purple rustling stems to the bank, stretched its neck to the water, drank, and lay still – a big cobra with fixed, lidless eyes.

'I have no stick – I have no stick,' said Kim. 'I will get me one and break his back.'

'Why? He is upon the Wheel as we are – a life ascending or descending – very far from deliverance. Great evil must the soul have done that is cast into this shape.'

'I hate all snakes,' said Kim. No native training can quench the white man's horror of the Serpent.

'Let him live out his life.' The coiled thing hissed and half opened its hood. 'May thy release come soon, brother!' the lama continued placidly. 'Hast *thou* knowledge, by chance, of my River?'

'Never have I seen such a man as thou art,' Kim whispered, overwhelmed. 'Do the very snakes understand thy talk?'
'Who knows?' He passed within a foot of the cobra's poised head. It flattened itself among the dusty coils.
'Come thou!' he called over his shoulder.
'Not I,' said Kim. 'I go round.'
'Come. He does no hurt.'
Kim hesitated for a moment. The lama backed his order by some droned Chinese quotation which Kim took for a charm. He obeyed and bounded across the rivulet, and the snake, indeed, made no sign.
'Never have I seen such a man.' Kim wiped the sweat from his forehead (51-3).

5.2 COMMENTARY

The opening of Chapter 3 finds Kim and the lama outside Umballa, begining their walk to Benares.

Kipling is noted for his colourful and colloquial rendition of speech, both in his fiction and his poetry. This passage of dialogue reveals a writer who listened carefully and understood the tacit understandings and omissions of the spoken language. Here, Kim maintains the outer confidence which he has shown in the previous chapters, but the lama begins to emerge as a figure of great, if quiet, strength.

The immediate stimulus to speech is the anger of the market-gardener, with his threatening bamboo pole. The narrator tells us that Kim knows the 'breed' to which the market-gardener belongs, implying that he can be classified along with his dogs. The lama's language is different, but his understanding is the same. In the measured rhythms of repeated negatives, he instructs Kim in human nature: 'Such an one . . . is impolite to strangers, intemperate of speech and uncharitable.' Following his own pacifist persuasion, the lama tells the farmer that 'We go from these unblessed fields.' He warns Kim to avoid like behaviour, a warning which Kim does not follow. Instead, he makes use of the lama's status to frighten the man, and insults him by calling him 'Mali', a term which means a gardener working for wages.

The narrator refers to the 'quiet dignity' of the lama. Later the lama 'placidly' blesses the cobra. The lama's dignity contrasts with the violent speech of the market-gardener, who forcefully reiterates the word 'beggars', and tells them to 'Begone!.' The combination of Kim's threats and the lama's quietness disturbs the gardener, and he begins to weaken, first entering into discussion about his canal, and then offering 'Milk and a meal', by which time he is stammering. 'It runs as straight as an arrow', he says of his canal, an image which recalls the lama's quest for the river of the arrow. But this canal, which costs as much as 'molten silver', is not the object of the search.

The lama continues to teach Kim in front of the gardener, warning Kim against anger, and then blessing the fields, which he had previously described as 'unblessed'. Always optimistic, the lama now sees the man as affable and courteous, while Kim again seizes the opportunity to assert himself, telling the gardener that he is lucky not to be cursed by the lama, and then walking off with his nose in the air. After a pause, the lama feels the need to warn Kim against the sin of pride, reminding him that all men are upon the Wheel.

Throughout this first part of the passage, Kim's attitude to life is contrasted with that of the lama. He is constantly seeking to score points, and uses the lama's own word 'discourteous' in extenuation. The lama reminds him that the gardener has withdrawn the discourtesy, and that this must be accepted. He also takes issue with Kim's description of the man as low-caste, another insult, and sharply and compactly asks: 'how can that be which is not?' If there is no caste, the word is meaningless.

The lama is not deceived about men and their motives. He tells Kim that the gardener was blinded by the 'Red Mist of anger'. The use of capitals is always a sign of the importance of an abstract concept to Kipling, and he uses it here for the River, the Middle Way and the Wheel of Things, as well as for the Serpent. The lama is well aware that the gardener, although like himself bound to the Wheel, 'does not tread the way of deliverance'. He reacts in the same way to the cobra, who is 'very far from deliverance', and must have done 'great evil' to get into this shape.

In the two paragraphs which fall between the main events of the passage, Kim asks the lama how he hopes to find his river. With his usual placidity, the lama tells him that enlightenment will come. In accordance with his promise, he blesses the gardener's river.

In the second part of the passage, Kim is terrified by a cobra, but the lama merely blesses it. Kipling draws a contrast between British and Indian behaviour, seeing the instinctive fear of the snake as a sign of the white man. The two episodes are closely connected, and one repeats the lessons of the other. Kim reacts strongly to the snake, as he has to the gardener. Following his training, he wants to find a stick and kill it. The lama's reaction is to remind Kim that the cobra too is upon the Wheel, and to bless it, calling it 'brother'. As with the canal, he asks the snake if he has knowledge of the sacred river.

The passage ends with the lama persuading Kim to jump over the snake. There is an implied comparison here with the episode in Chapter 9 when Lurgan fails to hypnotise Kim. The lama does not need to hypnotise the boy, whose confidence in him is complete. Recognising the lama's affinity with the natural world, Kim even wonders whether he can be understood by snakes. He is impressed by the lama's Chinese prayer, which he thinks might be a magic charm. The narrator suspends judgement. 'The snake, indeed, made no sign', leaves open the issue whether the snake has 'indeed' been influenced by the lama's prayer.

The passage exhibits many of the characteristic features of Kipling's prose. There is considerable use of alliteration, 'behind', 'brandished', 'bamboo'; 'disregarding the dogs'; 'milk and a meal'; 'shade of some tall sugar cane'; 'But be thou blessed to make the fields bear'. This, with the frequent repetition of key terms, 'we go', 'pride', 'I have no stick', gives even such an apparently straightforward passage of narrative something of a ritual effect. This impression is deepened by the formality of the lama's address, 'Afterwards he amended the discourtesy and I forgot the offence'; by archaisms, 'sought', 'forsooth', 'Begone' and 'hearthstone to byre' (cow-house), and by inversions 'well Kim knew', 'Is he not wise and holy'.

6 CRITICAL RECEPTION

6.1 CONTEMPORARY REVIEWS

Kim was greeted with immediate enthusiasm, and even, in some quarters, with relief. 'Take it or leave it has been his attitude from the first. In his own good time, after people had despaired of him, he wrote *Kim*', was the comment of one critic in the *New York Bookman*. To the *Times* critic, the novel represented a marked advance upon *Plain Tales from the Hills* and *The Day's Work*, standing to the earlier tales 'as a finished picture stands to a sketch'. 'His most ambitious and elaborate work . . . There is fascination, almost magic, in every page of the delightful volume', was the verdict in *Blackwood's Magazine*.

Most reviewers seized upon the picture of India for particular praise. 'Mr Kipling in *Kim* in *Cassell's Magazine* is once more the Mr Kipling who first won our hearts. His theme is India, where he is always at his best; and we learn more of the populace, the sects, the races, the lamas, the air, the sounds, scent and smells from a few pages than from libraries of learned authors', pronounced *Longman's Magazine*. The reviewer in *Blackwood's Magazine* particularly pointed to the description of the Grand Trunk Road as an instance of Kipling's 'patient industry', 'protracted observation' and 'thorough knowledge'. 'That he knew much of native life we were aware already, but how much he knew we had not – perhaps have not yet – fathomed.'

The same critic also praised the central creation of Kim himself: 'incomparably fresh and true: full of the delight of the artificer in the work of his hands, of the joy that comes from nothing so much as from the sense of successful achievement'. The other major characters represent a 'portrait-gallery of unusual extent and interest'. 'You do not stop to inquire whether he or any else is true to life. You *know* they are; you accept them all without question or reservation or cavil.' Only the stock figures of Father Victor and Bennett prevented Kipling from achieving perfection.

For the *Times* critic, as for Edmund Wilson forty years later, it was clear that Kim was destined for the Great Game, not for the Way. To this writer, the ending was 'pathetic' with the lama near death. He expressed a forlorn wish for a sequel. 'May we hope that another volume may speedily show us how he [Kim] fares in the years that follow?' The *Bookman* critic of 1902, gloomily noted the unevenness of the author's achievement, an enduring source of regret among writers on Kipling ever since. After *Kim* 'We told him distinctly that was the kind of thing we wanted of him, and asked him to do it again; whereupon he undertook the conduct of the British government through the agency of bad verse'.

One reviewer of *Kim* praised Lockwood Kipling's illustrations: 'of (to our mind) superlative excellence'. Lockwood Kipling himself:

> thought the notices on the whole . . . pretty good – very good indeed. You shouldn't pump (hot) water unawares upon a gracious public full of nerves – and *Kim* is in some respects pretty considerable a douche – so Indian, so remote, and in appearance so uncaring for the ordinary reader. The kind of reviewer who finds fault because it is what it sets out to be and not a carefully constructed drama with a plot and finale as the *Daily Chronicle* man – is pretty futile. But I thought there were some honest attempts to see eye to eye with the writer – which is one attitude a fair reviewer adopts.
>
> A. W. Baldwin, 'John Lockwood Kipling', in *Rudyard Kipling: the Man, his Work and his World*, ed. J. Gross (1972)

Among those who found fault with *Kim* was the first reviewer of the *Bookman*, Arthur Bartlett Maurice, writing in 1901. He began by preferring the book to Kipling's recent poetry, but went on to condemn it:

And there you have *Kim*, a jumble of native phrases, of extraneous conversations, of Eastern mysticism, redeemed and brought into a certain concrete form by that craft which Mr Kipling could not fail to acquire in the years of his apprenticeship and of his genius. It is all so cold, so dead, so lifeless. Mr Kipling seems to have gone raking through the cinders of his youth in search of the bits of half-burned coals with which to make a little flame and warmth. The spontaneous fire seems to have irrevocably gone.

Bookman (New York), XIV (October 1901)

6.2 LATER CRITICISMS

Kipling's reputation had already fallen before his death in 1936. He was popularly associated with imperialism and with extreme conservatism, and it was many years before he could be viewed as a writer rather than as a political scapegoat. The most enduring of the attacks are probably the series of parodies and caricatures by Max Beerbohm, who deeply disliked Kipling, and poked fun at what he saw as Kipling's warmongering, vulgarity and insensitivity. Among the first of the more sensitive critics was Bonamy Dobrée, writing in 1929. Dobrée sets the pattern for the future by excepting *Kim* from censure of the 'didactic' and 'moralist' in Kipling's writing: 'when his intuition was whole, as in *Kim*, in which the artist conquers the moralist and buries him deep under ground, he is nothing short of superb: his symbols clothe his intuition so that we take it for flesh and blood'.

In 1941, five years after Kipling's death, two important critical studies were published, both, in their different ways, establishing Kipling as an appropriate subject for literary analysis. The authors were both Americans, one a leading literary critic, Edmund Wilson (1895–1972), the other the poet, T. S. Eliot (1888–1965). Wilson's essay, 'The Kipling that Nobody Read', directed attention to the dark side of Kipling's work, and particularly to the late stories. Wilson, like many who followed him, presented Kipling as psychologically scarred by the Southsea episode. Rejecting the writer's own statement that those desperate years had drained him of hatred for life, Wilson argued that Kipling's work is 'shot through with hatred'.

For Wilson *Kim* is 'Kipling's only successful long story', 'an enchanting, almost a first-rate book, the work in which more perhaps than in any other he gave the sympathies of the imagination free rein to remember and to explore, and which has in consequence more complexity and density than any of his other works'. What prevents *Kim* from becoming a 'first-rate book' is, in Wilson's view, the lack of real conflict. The two worlds of India and of the British exist 'side by side, with neither really understanding the other, and we have watched the oscillations of Kim, as he passes to and fro between them. But the parallel lines never meet; the alternating attractions felt by Kim never give rise to a genuine struggle'. The novel has a double ending. The lama finds his river; Kim is promoted in the secret service. Kim chooses the British, and Kipling seems unaware that this is a betrayal of the lama. Once again, Kipling has chosen the strong, and abandoned the weak.

At first sight, T. S. Eliot seems an unexpected champion for Kipling, but his introduction to *A Choice of Kipling's Verse*, first published in 1941, has become a milestone in the Kipling revival. Eliot's main contention is that Kipling is a 'great verse writer' rather than a poet, and his chief concern in the introduction is with Kipling's poetry. Even so, he gives some attention to the prose, and writes of *Kim* as Kipling's 'maturest work on India, and his greatest book'. Eliot sees Kipling as an intuitive interpreter of India: 'it is the four great Indian characters in *Kim* who are real: the Lama, Mahbub Ali, Hurree Chunder Mookerjee, and the wealthy widow from the North . . . the first condition of understanding a foreign country is to smell it, as you smell India in *Kim*. If you have seen and felt truly, then if God has given you the power you may be able to think rightly'.

Those writers who immediately followed Eliot tried to understand what the obscure poet of the modern movement could see in the 'populariser' of Empire. Having answered their own question by rating them both as conservatives and outsiders, they then attacked. Boris Ford, writing in *Scrutiny* in 1942, quotes from Eliot's praise of *Kim*, which Ford is able only to damn with faint praise:

> This novel is so disarmingly superficial that even its less pleasant elements, those relating to the colour conflict, fail to give any sharp offence. And if indeed it seems to be one of his most satisfactory works, that is because the author's main interest is still . . . that of the boggle-eyed and fascinated initiate, and not yet that of the legislator.
>
> *Scrutiny*, XI, No. 1 (1942)

Ford denies that Kipling displays 'genuine sympathy' for the Indians in *Kim*, seeing the climax of the book as Kim's 'assertion of superiority', resulting in a 'willingness to use his Hindu affiliations in the service of the white foreigners'.

In the same year, in an essay displaying his customary blend of detachment and passion, George Orwell, began by insisting 'Kipling *is* a jingo imperialist, he *is* morally insensitive and aesthetically disgusting. It is better to start by admitting that, and then to try to find out why it is that he survives while the refined people who have sniggered at him seem to wear so badly.' Orwell does not discuss *Kim*, but his perceptive remark that 'some streak in him [Kipling] that may have been partly neurotic led him to prefer the active to the sensitive man' has a direct bearing on the central issues of the novel.

Another great American critic, Lionel Trilling (1905–75), in an essay of 1943, again accepts that *Kim* is Kipling's 'best book', if with an important proviso. He is referring here to his own reading of the book in childhood:

> Indians naturally have no patience whatever with Kipling and they condemn even his best book, *Kim*, saying that even here, where his devotion to the Indian life is most fully expressed, he falsely represents the Indians. Perhaps this is so, yet the dominant emotions of *Kim* are love and respect for the aspects of Indian life that the ethos of the West does not usually regard even with leniency. *Kim* established the value of things a boy was not likely to find approved anywhere else – the rank, greasy over-rich things, the life that was valuable outside the notions of orderliness, success, and gentility. It suggested not only a multitude of different ways of life, but even different modes of thought. Thus, whatever one might come to feel

personally about religion, a reading of *Kim* could not fail to establish religion's factual reality, not as piety, which was the apparent extent of its existence in the West, but as something at the very root of life.

Nation (New York), 16 October 1943

Trilling's recognition of the 'religious' element in *Kim* represents an important stage in the novel's critical history. Wilson also recognises the importance of Buddhism to Kipling. Wilson rightly identifies this as a connection between *Kim* and Kipling's later stories: 'it is certainly with Buddhism that we first find associated a mystical side of Kipling's mind which, in this last phase, is to emerge into the foreground'.

Trilling's assertion that Indians do not like *Kim* is challenged by Nirad C. Chaudhuri in an essay of 1957, to which he gives the provocative title: 'The Finest Story about India – in English'. Chaudhuri prefers to ignore Kipling's politics, and to see the spy story as an irrelevance, and to concentrate instead on Kipling's success in conveying the quality, the timelessness, of India itself. He sees Kipling's choice of a Tibetan lama, rather than a Hindu, to represent Indian religious life as a result of the writer's wish to separate active life from 'perfect beatitude and mystic quietism'. 'So he created his Lama, mixing Christianity with Buddhism'.

The first major modern study of Kipling as a writer was published by J.M.S. Tompkins in 1959. In an intelligent and perceptive passage on *Kim*, Dr Tompkins pinpoints a lack of conflict, and presents her own view of the 'open' ending. 'While, however, the threads are plaited together all through the book, they cannot be said to be drawn into a master-knot. One cannot replace the missing choice of Kim by an ordeal of the lama. It is not his love for Kim that provides the crisis . . . Yet, because the lama's love is the most important of the things that Kim comes to know, its consummation makes the end of the book'.

The most penetrating study of *Kim* is to be found in 'Vision in Kipling's Novels' by Mark Kinkead-Weekes, published in 1964 in *Kipling's Mind and Art*, edited by Andrew Rutherford. Kinkead-Weekes describes *Kim* as a carefully erected structure of conflicts and contrasts, seeing it as 'the answer to nine-tenths of the charges levelled against Kipling and the refutation of most of the generalisations about him'. For Kinkead-Weekes, the 'Great Game' plot is certainly inferior to the lama plot, and he reaches the opposite conclusion to Wilson, believing that, after his experience with the lama, Kim will be unable to join the secret service.

A number of general studies of Kipling contain valuable insights into *Kim*, among them Robert F. Moss's *Rudyard Kipling and the Fiction of Adolescence*, which relates *Kim* to *The Jungle Books*, *Stalky and Co.* and *Captains Courageous*. Alan Sandison's *The Wheel of Empire* (1967) places Kipling in the context of political theory, and the same author's introduction to the Oxford World's Classics edition of *Kim* is a fine analysis of the novel's meaning.

REVISION QUESTIONS

1. How much does *Kim* tell us about life in late nineteenth-century India?

2. From a reading of *Kim*, what would you suppose to be Kipling's attitude to racial and/or religious differences?

3. In what ways does Kipling develop Kim's character through the course of the novel?

4. Why does Kim question his own identity?

5. Compare Kipling's treatment of the characters of the lama and of Mahbub Ali.

6. How does Kipling make us believe in the goodness of the lama?

7. How does Kipling parallel and contrast the two 'quests' of Kim and the lama?

8. Discuss Kipling's treatment of the theme of fatherhood in *Kim*.

9. What is the significance of two of the following in *Kim*: the Wheel, the Road; the Way; the Great Game; caste; the sahib; the hills.

10. What part do women characters play in *Kim*?

11. Write on *Kim* as a 'journey novel'.

12. Indicate some of the ways in which Kipling draws attention to different languages in *Kim*.

13. How would you characterise Kipling as a writer of prose?

14. *Kim* has been described as 'pictorial'. What kind of pictures do you find in it?

15. Does the ending of *Kim* leave the reader 'up in the air'?

FURTHER READING

Kim is published in paperback by Macmillan; Pan in association with Macmillan; and Oxford University Press, World's Classics.

C. Carrington, *Rudyard Kipling, His Life and Work* (London: Macmillan, 1955, reprinted by Penguin Books, 1970).
N. C. Chaudhuri, 'The Finest Story About India – in English', in J. Gross (ed.) *Rudyard Kipling: the Man, his Work and his World* (London: Weidenfeld & Nicolson, 1972) pp. 27–35. First published in *Encounter*, XIII, 4 (April 1957) pp. 47–53.
E. L. Gilbert (ed.) *Kipling and the Critics* (London: Peter Owen, 1966).
R. Lancelyn Green (ed.) *Kipling: the Critical Heritage* (London: Routledge, 1971).
P. Mason, *Kipling: The Glass, the Shadow and the Fire* (London: Jonathan Cape, 1975).
R. F. Moss, *Rudyard Kipling and the Fiction of Adolescence* (London: Macmillan, 1982).
M. Kinkead-Weekes, 'Vision in Kipling's Novels' in A. Rutherford (ed.) *Kipling's Mind and Art*, (London: Oliver & Boyd, 1964) pp. 197–234.
R. Kipling, *Something of Myself* (London: Macmillan, 1937).
A. Mason (Brigadier) 'Kim', in *The Reader's Guide to Kipling's Work* (privately printed for the Kipling Society, 1961) pp. 119–269.
P. Mudford, *Birds of a Different Plumage: A Study of British-Indian Relations From Akbar to Curzon* (London: Collins, 1974).

T. Pinney, *Kipling's India: Uncollected Sketches, 1884–88* (London: Macmillan, 1986).

A. Sandison, 'Rudyard Kipling: The Imperial Simulacrum', in his *The Wheel of Empire* (London: Macmillan, 1967) pp. 64–119.

J. I. M. Stewart, *Rudyard Kipling* (London: Gollancz, 1966).

J. M. S. Tompkins, *The Art of Rudyard Kipling* (London: Methuen, 1959).

A. Wilson, *The Strange Ride of Rudyard Kipling* (London: Secker & Warburg, 1977).

Works by Rudyard Kipling (selected works)

1886 *Departmental Ditties*
1888 *Plain Tales from the Hills*
1890 *The Light that Failed*
1891 *Life's Handicap*
1892 *Barrack-Room Ballads; The Naulahka* (with Wolcott Balestier)
1893 *Many Inventions*
1894 *The Jungle Book*
1895 *The Second Jungle Book*
1896 *The Seven Seas*
1897 *Captains Courageous*
1898 *The Day's Work*
1899 *Stalky and Co.*
1901 *Kim*
1902 *Just So Stories*
1903 *The Five Nations*
1904 *Traffics and Discoveries*
1906 *Puck of Pook's Hill*
1909 *Actions and Reactions*
1910 *Rewards and Fairies*
1913 *Letters of Travel; Songs from Books*
1917 *A Diversity of Creatures*
1919 *The Years Between*
1923 *Land and Sea Tales; The Irish Guards in the Great War*
1926 *Debits and Credits*

1927 *Brazilian Sketches*
1928 *A Book of Words*
1930 *Thy Servant a Dog*
1932 *Limits and Renewals*
1937 *Something of Myself*

Mastering English Literature
Richard Gill

Mastering English Literature will help readers both to enjoy English Literature and to be successful in 'O' levels, 'A' levels and other public exams. It is an introduction to the study of poetry, novels and drama which helps the reader in four ways - by providing ways of approaching literature, by giving examples and practice exercises, by offering hints on how to write about literature, and by the author's own evident enthusiasm for the subject. With extracts from more than 200 texts, this is an enjoyable account of how to get the maximum satisfaction out of reading, whether it be for formal examinations or simply for pleasure.

Work Out English Literature ('A' level)
S.H. Burton

This book familiarises 'A' level English Literature candidates with every kind of test which they are likely to encounter. Suggested answers are worked out step by step and accompanied by full author's commentary. The book helps students to clarify their aims and establish techniques and standards so that they can make appropriate responses to similar questions when the examination pressures are on. It opens up fresh ways of looking at the full range of set texts, authors and critical judgements and motivates students to know more of these matters.

Also from Macmillan
CASEBOOK SERIES

The Macmillan *Casebook* series brings together the best of modern criticism with a selection of early reviews and comments. Each Casebook charts the development of opinion on a play, poem, or novel, or on a literary genre, from its first appearance to the present day.

GENERAL THEMES

COMEDY: DEVELOPMENTS IN CRITICISM
D. J. Palmer

DRAMA CRITICISM: DEVELOPMENTS SINCE IBSEN
A. J. Hinchliffe

THE ENGLISH NOVEL: DEVELOPMENTS IN CRITICISM SINCE HENRY JAMES
Stephen Hazell

THE LANGUAGE OF LITERATURE
N. Page

THE PASTORAL MODE
Bryan Loughrey

THE ROMANTIC IMAGINATION
J. S. Hill

TRAGEDY: DEVELOPMENTS IN CRITICISM
R. P. Draper

POETRY

WILLIAM BLAKE: SONGS OF INNOCENCE AND EXPERIENCE
Margaret Bottrall

BROWNING: MEN AND WOMEN AND OTHER POEMS
J. R. Watson

BYRON: CHILDE HAROLD'S PILGRIMAGE AND DON JUAN
John Jump

CHAUCER: THE CANTERBURY TALES
J. J. Anderson

COLERIDGE: THE ANCIENT MARINER AND OTHER POEMS
A. R. Jones and W. Tydeman

DONNE: SONGS AND SONETS
Julian Lovelock

T. S. ELIOT: FOUR QUARTETS
Bernard Bergonzi

T. S. ELIOT: PRUFROCK, GERONTION, ASH WEDNESDAY AND OTHER POEMS
B. C. Southam

T. S. ELIOT: THE WASTELAND
C. B. Cox and A. J. Hinchliffe

ELIZABETHAN POETRY: LYRICAL AND NARRATIVE
Gerald Hammond

THOMAS HARDY: POEMS
J. Gibson and T. Johnson

GERALD MANLEY HOPKINS: POEMS
Margaret Bottrall

KEATS: ODES
G. S. Fraser

KEATS: THE NARRATIVE POEMS
J. S. Hill

MARVELL: POEMS
Arthur Pollard

THE METAPHYSICAL POETS
Gerald Hammond

MILTON: PARADISE LOST
A. E. Dyson and Julian Lovelock

POETRY OF THE FIRST WORLD WAR
Dominic Hibberd

ALEXANDER POPE: THE RAPE OF THE LOCK
John Dixon Hunt

SHELLEY: SHORTER POEMS & LYRICS
Patrick Swinden

SPENSER: THE FAERIE QUEEN
Peter Bayley

TENNYSON: IN MEMORIAM
John Dixon Hunt

THIRTIES POETS: 'THE AUDEN GROUP'
Ronald Carter

WORDSWORTH: LYRICAL BALLADS
A. R. Jones and W. Tydeman

WORDSWORTH: THE PRELUDE
W. J. Harvey and R. Gravil

W. B. YEATS: POEMS 1919-1935
E. Cullingford

W. B. YEATS: LAST POEMS
Jon Stallworthy

THE NOVEL AND PROSE

JANE AUSTEN: EMMA
David Lodge

JANE AUSTEN: NORTHANGER ABBEY AND PERSUASION
B. C. Southam

JANE AUSTEN: SENSE AND SENSIBILITY, PRIDE AND PREJUDICE AND MANSFIELD PARK
B. C. Southam

CHARLOTTE BRONTË: JANE EYRE AND VILLETTE
Miriam Allott

EMILY BRONTË: WUTHERING HEIGHTS
Miriam Allott

BUNYAN: THE PILGRIM'S PROGRESS
R. Sharrock

CONRAD: HEART OF DARKNESS, NOSTROMO AND UNDER WESTERN EYES
C. B. Cox

CONRAD: THE SECRET AGENT
Ian Watt

CHARLES DICKENS: BLEAK HOUSE
A. E. Dyson

CHARLES DICKENS: DOMBEY AND SON AND LITTLE DORRITT
Alan Shelston

CHARLES DICKENS: HARD TIMES, GREAT EXPECTATIONS AND OUR MUTUAL FRIEND
N. Page

GEORGE ELIOT: MIDDLEMARCH
Patrick Swinden

GEORGE ELIOT: THE MILL ON THE FLOSS AND SILAS MARNER
R. P. Draper

HENRY FIELDING: TOM JONES
Neil Compton

E. M. FORSTER: A PASSAGE TO INDIA
Malcolm Bradbury

HARDY: THE TRAGIC NOVELS
R. P. Draper

HENRY JAMES: WASHINGTON SQUARE AND THE PORTRAIT OF A LADY
Alan Shelston

JAMES JOYCE: DUBLINERS AND A PORTRAIT OF THE ARTIST AS A YOUNG MAN
Morris Beja

D. H. LAWRENCE: THE RAINBOW AND WOMEN IN LOVE
Colin Clarke

D. H. LAWRENCE: SONS AND LOVERS
Gamini Salgado

SWIFT: GULLIVER'S TRAVELS
Richard Gravil

THACKERAY: VANITY FAIR
Arthur Pollard

TROLLOPE: THE BARSETSHIRE NOVELS
T. Bareham

VIRGINIA WOOLF: TO THE LIGHTHOUSE
Morris Beja

DRAMA

CONGREVE: COMEDIES
Patrick Lyons

T. S. ELIOT: PLAYS
Arnold P. Hinchliffe

JONSON: EVERY MAN IN HIS HUMOUR AND THE ALCHEMIST
R. V. Holdsworth

JONSON: VOLPONE
J. A. Barish

MARLOWE: DR FAUSTUS
John Jump

MARLOWE: TAMBURLAINE, EDWARD II AND THE JEW OF MALTA
John Russell Brown

MEDIEVAL ENGLISH DRAMA
Peter Happé

O'CASEY: JUNO AND THE PAYCOCK, THE PLOUGH AND THE STARS AND THE SHADOW OF A GUNMAN
R. Ayling

JOHN OSBORNE: LOOK BACK IN ANGER
John Russell Taylor

WEBSTER: THE WHITE DEVIL AND THE DUCHESS OF MALFI
R. V. Holdsworth

WILDE: COMEDIES
W. Tydeman

SHAKESPEARE

SHAKESPEARE: ANTONY AND CLEOPATRA
John Russell Brown

SHAKESPEARE: CORIOLANUS
B. A. Brockman

SHAKESPEARE: HAMLET
John Jump

SHAKESPEARE: HENRY IV PARTS I AND II
G. K. Hunter

SHAKESPEARE: HENRY V
Michael Quinn

SHAKESPEARE: JULIUS CAESAR
Peter Ure

SHAKESPEARE: KING LEAR
Frank Kermode

SHAKESPEARE: MACBETH
John Wain

SHAKESPEARE: MEASURE FOR MEASURE
G. K. Stead

SHAKESPEARE: THE MERCHANT OF VENICE
John Wilders

SHAKESPEARE: A MIDSUMMER NIGHT'S DREAM
A. W. Price

SHAKESPEARE: MUCH ADO ABOUT NOTHING AND AS YOU LIKE IT
John Russell Brown

SHAKESPEARE: OTHELLO
John Wain

SHAKESPEARE: RICHARD II
N. Brooke

SHAKESPEARE: THE SONNETS
Peter Jones

SHAKESPEARE: THE TEMPEST
D. J. Palmer

SHAKESPEARE: TROILUS AND CRESSIDA
Priscilla Martin

SHAKESPEARE: TWELFTH NIGHT
D. J. Palmer

SHAKESPEARE: THE WINTER'S TALE
Kenneth Muir